The Merriman Chronicles

Book Six

The Threat in the Americas

Copyright Information

The Merriman Chronicles - Book 6

The Threat in the Americas

Copyright © 2015 by Roger Burnage

With the exception of certain well known historical figures, the characters in this book have no relation or resemblance to any person living or dead.

All rights reserved. This book and all "The Merriman Chronicles" are works of fiction. No part of this book may be reproduced or used in any manner without written permission of the copyright owner except for the use of quotations in a book review.

2025 Edition

Updated by: Robin Burnage
Edited by: Katharine D'Souza
Cover painting by: Colin M Baxter

ISBN: 9798317217396 (Paperback)
ISBN: 9798317310080 (Hardcover)

www.merriman-chronicles.com

Books in the series

James Abel Merriman (1768 – 1843)

A Certain Threat
The Threat in the West Indies
The French Invasion
The Threat in the East
The Threat in the Baltic
The Threat in the Americas
The Threat in the Adriatic
The Threat in the Atlantic

Edward James Merriman (1853 - 1928)

The Fateful Voyage

Preface

The year was 1799, in early spring.

Captain Brough was a worried man. The gales had been almost ceaseless for over seven days, blowing the ship ever closer to the coast of northern Brazil. Because of the value of the cargo he had been ordered to keep well away from the threat of privateers as well as the French and Spanish frigates attacking British trading ships. After rounding Cape of Good Hope with its high seas and strong winds with no damage to the ship, Captain Brough had taken his ship far out into the Atlantic Ocean, maybe two hundred miles or more off the coast. No other ships had been sighted and there had been no problems until the gales had started.

In the interest of as fast a passage as possible he had been overconfident. The ship carried too much sail overnight and that first and unexpected gale had caused terrible damage aloft when it struck at first light, laying her over until the mainyard almost touched the sea. The fore and main topgallant masts had gone, taking the topmasts with them. Men had gone overboard trapped and tangled in the torn sails and rigging with no hope of rescue. Desperate work with axes and knives had managed to free the ship from the encumbrances and she had again rolled upright, but since then the ship could do no more than run precariously before the wind and waves.

Finally the weather eased. Fore and aft sails had been rigged from the fore lower mast and the stump of the mainmast which, together with the spanker on the mizzen mast, enabled some control to be taken over the ship's progress. Despite this, the coast of Brazil was soon sighted. The terrified passengers were able to come on deck at last and it was hoped that the ship could anchor somewhere where fresh water could be found, perhaps even some village where provisions could be bought.

Thankfully a small town was sighted and the ship anchored close to shore in a bay where a river emptied itself into the sea.

The town was little more than a village surrounding the remains of a small fort. There were only a few inhabitants who could do little to help other than sell some vegetables and chickens to help eke out the ship's dwindling supplies. The water casks were refilled from the river but nobody had ventured far from the town whose people warned of attacks from native people in the lush rainforest. Indeed, the locals themselves had been attacked and dared not go out to tend the sugar and tobacco plantations inland.

Eventually Captain Brough decided that they would have to try and reach somewhere to the north where suitable timber might be found to replace the masts, or at least the topmasts, and so preparations were made to leave the next morning. At first light, the depleted crew set about raising the few sails but there was no wind. The sea was like a mirror and the heat oppressive.

As the men looked helplessly about, the sea suddenly began to recede until the ship grounded. Before anyone was able to react, a massive wave, higher than the mizzen mast, was spotted approaching the shore. The captain had only moments to shout, "Tidal wave! Hold on for your lives," before the water struck. The ship was lifted bodily and carried inland, crashing into forest trees which were themselves smashed by the water. The water receded a little before another wave carried the ship further inland where it crashed down on rocks and broke in half.

Chapter One

Southward bound, late 1801

The autumnal gales had almost ceased as the small flotilla sailed south towards the equator, bound for the Brazilian coast. Captain Sir James Merriman sat in his great cabin aboard the frigate *Lord Stevenage* and once again read his orders from the Admiralty. French and Spanish frigates had been commerce raiding in the south Atlantic, probably many of them were privateers and no British ships were safe. His orders were to sail as far south as the Rio de la Plata in the hope of finding and disposing of as many of the enemy ships as he could.

He was reminded that, in August 1800, a convoy of valuable East Indiamen had had been subject to an attempted attack by a French frigate force off the north east coast of Brazil. The only naval escort was HMS *Belliqueux*, a ship of the line, under Captain Rowley Bulteel. Fortunately the Indiamen were large, heavily armed ships which at a distance could be mistaken for ships of the line so that when they formed up into line of battle they frightened the French commander into turning tail and trying to escape. Turning from defence to attack, the Indiamen and HMS *Belliqueux* gave chase and captured two of the French ships.

Somewhat vague and unclear though they were, Merriman knew these orders from the Admiralty to proceed to the South Atlantic were only an initial start point. His passenger would have other orders for him when they got there. This passenger was a man by the name of George Humphries, part of the extensive network of English spies and agents controlled by a department of the Treasury. At that time they worked to seek out intelligence about England's enemies, particularly France, Spain and the new United States of America. Effectively the Lord Stevenage was seconded to the Treasury with Merriman in command of the ship, but it was Mr Humphries who would tell him where he was to go.

Merriman had been involved in this kind of work before and had built up a trust and friendship with another agent, Laurence Grahame, during their adventures in Ireland, the West Indies, India and the Baltic. The two of them were keen readers of Shakespeare's plays and had participated in friendly contest to see who could find a suitable quotation for any event or situation. Grahame had since been promoted to higher office at the Treasury and Merriman missed the friendly banter. Mr Humphries had taken his place but would not yet tell Merriman what his orders were.

Merriman went up on deck and looked astern at the small flotilla of two ships which were under his command. The biggest was a French corvette, a small frigate really, which he and his ship had captured last year. The ship had been dismasted in a gale then surrendered without a fight and Merriman had decided to tow it home to Portsmouth. It had been refitted by the English shipyard, a slow process due to the fact that so many of the Navy's ships needed work done to get them back to sea again as rapidly as possible. Most of them had spent months at sea on blockade duty off French ports and needed urgent work done. The corvette, renamed *Eagle* had been completed only a handful of days before the flotilla was ordered to the south Atlantic. The ship was commanded by newly promoted Post-Captain David Andrews. Prior to his promotion, Andrews had been with Merriman in each of his commands from the small brig *Conflict* and the sloop *Aphrodite* to being First Lieutenant aboard the frigate *Lord Stevenage*. Merriman trusted him implicitly and knew that he would quickly bring his new crew up to the required standard.

The other ship was a small brig, but the sight of it on station did nothing to improve Merriman's temper. During the voyage, in bad weather, strong winds and the calm of the doldrums, Merriman had exercised his ships and men regularly, in particular the speed of the other ships to reply to and execute his signals. He had visited the other two ships and put each of them through a series of moves including sail handling, gunnery and boat work, even boat races. The crews would be carrying out his orders when he changed them, meaning that men doing one task were suddenly ordered to do something different and another change of orders would interrupt them yet again.

In this he also exercised his own crew but they were so used to him finding something different to do in the middle of some exercise they were engaged in that only very rarely was there any confusion. Every man knew his position and duty at all times, even the new man, Lieutenant De Mowbray, was efficient in command of the starboard gundeck while Lieutenant Bristow commanded the larboard side of the gundeck. Mowbray, with three replacement seamen, had joined the ship at the last minute before the flotilla sailed. Those three had yet to prove themselves as good enough and able to come up to Merriman's stern standards. Indeed one of them, a surly rogue, was slow to obey his orders and was always quarrelling with his shipmates and petty officers.

Captain Andrews, with the knowledge gained over the years as Merriman's First Lieutenant, had managed during the long voyage south to train his crew up to Merriman's standards very well indeed. When Merriman stood with Andrews on the quarter deck of the corvette *The Eagle* he found very little to comment on. He smiled to himself as indeed he had not really expected to find anything.

But it was aboard the brig *The Mayfly* that he had cause for concern. The captain, Lieutenant Stewart, did not have the rapid speed of mind to adapt to the sudden changes of orders and the result was often confusion on deck. Merriman was disappointed at the slowness of the man to issue his own orders following Merriman's changes of order and the gunnery was appalling, slow and not fired together. Something would have to be done about it.

He had decided after much thought to speak with Stewart out of the hearing of his own crew so he passed the order for Stewart to come over to the *Lord Stevenage*. When the man duly arrived and was ushered into the great cabin he found Merriman seated at his desk reading the ship's log book. He stood there, not being invited to sit down, until Merriman turned to face him.

"Well, Mr Stewart, what have you to say for yourself? I am appalled at the inefficient way your officers and men carried out my orders. The delays and confusion on deck are unacceptable. Such confusion could result in your ship not able to meet an enemy ship, which in turn would result in failure in action especially as your gunnery is frankly laughable. I had thought that a man of your age and experience would do better."

Stewart had got red in the face and burst out with, "Sir, I am old for my rank because I spent too long ashore as Flag Officer to various Admirals with little sea time to learn about command. Before now I was in command of a cutter as messenger to the Fleet with no action to speak of. This is my first time in command of a real warship, sir, and, apart from a few good men, my crew are new, the sweepings of the dockyard and my warrant officers are not very experienced. One in particular is a bad influence on the men."

"Oh, and what is the problem with him?" asked Merriman.

"He mistreats the men, sir. He is abusing his position. He is far too ready to use his cane on any man who displeases him or who is too slow, with the result that the men have become sullen and resentful, especially the men new to the life who do try their best and are improving all the time. I have spoken to him several times about it, sir, but it seems to make little difference."

"I recommend, Mr Stewart, that you censure him again and threaten to dis-rate him back to seaman which you are perfectly entitled to do. If he goes back to being a seaman he will not have his blue jacket to protect him anymore and the threat of what the men may do to him may improve his attitude. You must assert your authority more. You are the captain after all and a captain's word is law on your ship."

"Yes, sir, thank you. I'll try that," replied Stewart.

"You will do more than try that. Lieutenant. You will enforce it. I understand your problem but it does not and cannot excuse the low standard of your ship's performance. I have decided that you will remain here whilst I show you how I expect your ship to be trained. Then I will send some of my warrant officers back to your ship with you together with my second Lieutenant Mr Shrigley. You will order your men to obey them as they would your own people. Is that clear? If you can't improve things I can have no use for *The Mayfly.*"

"Yes, sir," mumbled the man shamefacedly.

Merriman led the way on deck and called to the officer of the watch. "Mr Shrigley, clear for action, immediately."

Shrigley wasted no time, bawling orders which had men boiling up from below to take their stations at the guns and the topmen by the masts waiting for orders for sail handling. Banging from beneath the quarterdeck told of the partitions and furniture being taken below and officers' and midshipmen's chests taken to the orlop to form a table for the ship's doctor to deal with injured men and operate on.

The officers and midshipmen went straight to their appointed places, each ready to inform the Captain that his men were ready for anything. First Lieutenant Merryweather took his place with Merriman and the signal midshipmen aft by the signals locker. Before that first order was completed, Merriman ordered the courses - the big lower sails - to be furled and nets rigged overhead to protect men from any falling objects. Before that was done he shouted, "Belay that order. Fire has broken out below for'ard. Fire party, rig the water pump and get below." He waited for a few moments then shouted, "Prepare to repel boarders and ten men from the portside guns are dead. Captain St James, have your marines form an afterguard."

In spite of the conflicting and sometimes unexpected orders, the men moved purposefully. There was no confusion and Lieutenant Stewart watched in amazement.

"Lieutenant Merriweather, stand the men down now, normal duties and watches. Lieutenant Stewart, now you see what is expected from a well-trained crew. So, back to your ship with the men of mine that I have selected and I shall be looking for increased efficiency there. You will increase the frequency of training your crew especially at gunnery until I see a great deal of improvement."

"Aye-aye, sir. I'll do my best, count on it," he said and climbed down into his boat where Merriman's men were already waiting.

Since then, the standard of the crew of *The Mayfly* had improved remarkably. Shrigley and Merriman's men had returned some days later to report that they could do no more. The men reported on what they had done to sort out the other crew by moving some men to different positions and making them practice at the guns until they were near dropping. It was now up to Lieutenant Stewart to carry on with improving his crew's performance.

Chapter Two

Across the Equator

When the ships reached the equator, there was the usual visit aboard from King Neptune and his small entourage. Neptune was the bos'n wearing long hair and a beard made from teased out rope and sporting a cloak of canvas painted with pictures of fish and other sea creatures. His 'wife', a bos'n's mate, had a wig of long pieces of rope and a homemade dress puffed out in front by pieces of old canvas. They had two men with them to administer the rites of passage to those of the crew who had not previously crossed the equator.

It was usually a busy and hilarious occasion but this time most men aboard had been present when *Lord Stevenage* crossed the line on their last voyage to India. The ceremony did not last long as the only ones who had not been there before were two midshipmen, three men out of the crew and a marine. It was a simple affair, the six to be introduced to Neptune were stripped and dunked in the bight of a sail suspended over the gundeck filled with seawater and then made to kneel to the King who dished out various punishments. The midshipmen were dunked in the water twice more again and released but the three seamen were charged to climb to the highest point of the mainmast before climbing down to be doused in seawater again accompanied by raucous comments such as, *"Joe, at least you'll be nearly clean again,"* and *"Don't leave that one in too long, 'e's a skinny bugger and he might shrink"*. It was a race and the last man down was made to do the climb again. The marine was dunked repeatedly and then made to run the length of the ship before being thrown into the water again.

Merriman, who had endured the ceremony years before on his own first voyage to India, stood on the quarterdeck with the officers enjoying the spectacle. Amid the hilarity, the lookouts remained in place aloft, such was the discipline of the Navy. He knew that the men enjoyed the ceremony and he awarded Neptune and his people a double tot of rum and the rest of the crew a single tot each to close the event. "Three for Sir James and make 'em good 'uns," yelled an unknown voice, to which the entire crew responded with loud cheers and applause. Merriman acknowledged it all by raising his hat before going below.

The next morning, with the fun over, Captain Sir James Merriman stalked up and down the quarterdeck as was his usual custom at dawn and glowered at anyone foolish enough to come near him. Seeing his mood, nobody did. The men whose duty kept them there tried to appear as busy or as invisible as possible. The crew had prepared for battle, as was normal at dawn, but when no enemy ship was seen they stood down and prepared for their meagre breakfast. Merriman continued to pace up and down wearing his usual faded and salt-stained coat and white trousers, picking his way between ringbolts, the lashed guns, and coiled ropes. Long experience had taught him to miss all those various things, indeed he hardly noticed them.

Perhaps an hour later, Merriman, by now feeling the prickling of sweat beneath his shirt and running down his back, decided to go below for his servant Peters to shave him. Then he would have his breakfast. He had hardly reached his cabin before he heard a hail from a lookout aloft.

"Deck there, sail astern again."

That sail had been seen every day for the last three weeks, the same one certainly because the sail was a square sail but of an unusual shape, much narrower across the top than normal, but it always dropped back and disappeared. Merriman knew that if anything unusual happened he would be informed immediately, so he carried on with the routine of washing, shaving, changing into a clean pair of trousers and a clean shirt and then breakfasting.

His man Peters had been with him for years and, sensing Merriman's mood, carefully carried out his duties and said nothing. Merriman's mood was not improved when he looked at himself in the mirror Peters held up to him. He saw the usual tanned face with bright blue eyes and the dark hair tied back at the nape of his neck by a fashionable bow, but what upset him was the sight of a few grey hairs beginning to show at his temples. Damn it, but he was getting old. *Older*, he told himself, *happens to all of us,* but he was only thirty two years and resented seeing the grey hair.

Later, Merriman was thinking about his passenger Mr Humphries, the Treasury man. George Humphries was a tall, lean, dark-haired man who had quickly made himself popular with the officers with his affable manner, an endless repertoire of stories and his liking for a hard fought game of chess. He was so good at that game he now had difficulty in finding an opponent apart from Doctor McBride, the ship's surgeon, who was keen on a tricky game himself. Humphries was also able to coax a tune out of an old and rather battered set of pipes. Merriman had invited his officers, including Humphries, to dinner on two occasions and they had invited him to a meal in the wardroom, but he knew little more about the man than when he first came on board.

Damn and blast the man. I've had enough of his secrecy, thought Merriman. I'll have it out of him now!

Merriman told his servant Peters to pass the word that he wanted Mr Humphries in his cabin at once. He waited impatiently until the marine sentry thumped his musket on the deck and called, "Mr Humphries to see you, sir."

"Send him in," replied Merriman and took a seat behind his desk. "Sit down, sir. Now then, Mr Humphries, I have had enough of your secrecy about where we are going and what we may expect when we get there. Secrecy is fine in your line of business but we have no means of telling anyone what we are about, indeed we haven't seen another ship since we left England, other than some of our ships on blockade duty round the French coast. There was one ship which seemed to be following us, we saw him at dawn nearly every day then he wasn't seen for several days until he appeared again this morning. Is that ship part of your secrets?"

"No, Sir James, not as far as I know, but there are enemy spies in London and Portsmouth and news of our mission may have leaked out there."

"It's quite possible, sir. I have had dealings with French spies when I was with Sir Grahame in Ireland and other places, latterly the Baltic. He may have told you about our various adventures. We had a good friendship and he trusted me in all things. Why can't you do the same, tell me that?"

"Sir Grahame told me all about your missions and he also told me I could trust you completely. On my previous missions I have had to maintain the greatest secrecy and that has become a habit hard to break. I apologise for not speaking with you earlier but now I will tell you."

Merriman nodded with satisfaction.

"The first thing we are to do is to sail down to the area near the Rio de la Plata - we call it the River Plate - to see if anything can be learned about the Spanish warships and activities in the town of Montevideo. That is their main harbour in the River Plate. From vague reports it is thought that privateers down there are being organised by one man. That man is one Don Carlos Galiano, a Spaniard whom Sir Grahame has told me you know."

"I do indeed although I met him only once. He was behind the troubles in some of our islands in the Caribbean. He had a scheme of violence to force English settlers to leave so that he could buy their rich estates cheaply with their crops of sugar and coffee and everything else. His daughter and son-in-law were involved as well but they killed each other when we captured their ship. Their ships and the son's estate were full of stolen merchandise but Don Carlos disappeared and we never found him. So he has surfaced again, has he? He is a ruthless man, a criminal and a murderer and must be brought to justice."

"Well, sir, what you must do is put me ashore as close to those towns as you can. I am a fluent speaker of both Spanish and Portuguese and also French and can easily pass as a native of those countries. On the way there you must continue to carry out your orders from the Admiralty with regard to enemy ships."

Merriman nodded, glad to have some clarity of purpose at last.

Humphries held up a hand. "There is one other task we are expected to do."

Chapter Three

Humphries reveals the main mission

Humphries coughed to clear his throat and Merriman, now in a better humour, sat forward in his chair and called for Peters to bring coffee. When they were served from Merriman's dwindling store, Merriman motioned to Humphries to continue.

"Two years ago, maybe a bit more, an important Indiaman disappeared. It was assumed that she had gone down with all hands in some gale since nothing more was heard or seen of it. The ship had sailed from Calcutta with a rich cargo of silks and spices and other exotic goods including a chest full of precious stones and was to go as part of a convoy on her way back to England. She carried passengers as well as cargo, including two very important people from India who were to report back to the Prime Minister."

Merriman frowned, having heard nothing of this loss previously.

"Now, I said that nothing was heard of the ship. That was true until several weeks ago when a man by the name of Chalmers arrived back in London with an amazing tale to tell. He had been the first officer on board that ill-fated ship when the disaster happened. Apparently the ship was beset by powerful storms and was severely damaged before they found shelter in a bay and anchored at the mouth of a small river near a Portuguese town named Maceio or something like that. They had managed to effect some repairs and then, one morning as the ship was preparing to leave, an immense tidal wave lifted the ship and carried it inland up the river. Another wave followed which again lifted the ship and then it crashed down on rocks and broke in two."

"A terrible tale, sir. What happened next? How did this Chalmers fellow get back to London and how many survivors were there?"

"Apparently there were only a few. The captain had disappeared with many of the crew and most of the passengers too. Those that were still living began to repair the only boat left but it wasn't big enough to carry them all so a small party of armed men set off along the coast to try and find help. Only one man returned to tell that the rest of them had been killed by native Indians and he died soon after from his wounds. The boat would be overloaded but the survivors decided that they had no choice but to use it otherwise they may all be killed."

Humphries took another sip of his coffee and went on, "Chalmers said that the boat carried two women passengers, one of the important passengers, four crewmen and himself. They had only a small sail and they proceeded slowly northwards but saw no other ships. The two women and three of the crew eventually died and were put overboard then some days later Chalmers and the other two men were found by a trading vessel and taken to Antigua. All three were in a terrible state. Eventually both the others died and only Chalmers was left. He came back home on board another trader in a convoy escorted by the Navy. He reported to the East India Company offices and told them the bad news but he refused to accompany a rescue mission."

Both men sat silently for a few moments, Humphries shaking his head sadly and Merriman wondering what was yet to be told.

Humphries sighed and spoke again, "A sad tale, sir, but there is more. The Company advised my office at the Treasury and they in turn approached the Admiralty. Sir Laurence Grahame was most insistent that you were given this task which is why we are here."

"But what are we expected to do, Mr Humphries? Are we to find that ship and rescue the gems? It is not the usual thing the

Royal Navy is involved in, is it?"

"No, Sir James, it isn't, but beside the gems, which are of great value, there are some important documents concerning treaties with Indian rulers who are more prepared to toe the line now that Tippoo Sahib has been defeated and killed at Seringapatam. I believe you were in India yourself, sir, at the time. The documents must be retrieved if at all possible and that is the principal reason for this mission."

"Indeed, I was there with Mr Grahame, as he was then, but surely any documents will have been destroyed by seawater when the ship was smashed on the rocks."

"Quite possibly so, sir, but they were sealed in waxed paper in the strong chest of precious stones and stored in a locker beneath the stern windows of the Captain's cabin. Mr Chalmers knew the chest was there because he and the Captain brought it on board secretly and concealed it. He also said he believed that it was still there in spite of the extensive damage to the ship."

"And which comes first, sir, our voyage to South America looking for enemies or to find the shipwreck?" asked Merriman.

"The voyage down to at least as far as the River Plate, Sir James. After all, if we found the chest first and then lost this ship the documents could be lost for ever."

"Very well, Mr Humphries, that is what we must do, but I must advise my officers of our plan. I will call Captains Andrews and Stewart aboard. When they arrive I will have all my officers together and you can relate to them the entire story. Now then, there is something else you are keeping from me. What is in the two chests that you brought aboard my ship?"

"Nothing of value, sir. Just some cheap items that we might need to trade with any natives we find in Brazil but if I may suggest, nobody should be told of the gems, only that we are to look for a small chest of important documents."

"I understand. Now I must change into uniform and we must go on deck."

On deck Merriman called the lieutenant of the watch, Mr Bristow, to him. "Mr Bristow, heave to if you please and have your midshipman signal to the other ships ordering them to heave to as well. Their Captains are to come aboard at once."

"Aye-aye, sir," replied the officer, turning to bawl the necessary orders to the signal midshipman, Mr Green, and to the men to back the topsails to bring the ship to a standstill where she lay, rolling gently to the small swell.

Merriman watched everything with his usual keen eye while he waited for Captain Andrews of the corvette *Eagle* and the captain of the brig *The Mayfly,* Lieutenant Stewart to arrive. He did not have long to wait. The men were soon in their boats with their crews pulling furiously to try and get their officer first to the frigate. Both officers could be seen in full uniform, hastily fastening buttons and settling their hats and swords correctly.

They arrived almost together but Lieutenant Stewart had to wait until Captain Andrews boarded first as befitted his rank. His arrival was marked with all the ceremony so beloved by the Navy, the bos'n's whistles and the stamp of the marines' boots on the deck as they presented arms in a cloud of dusty pipeclay. The marine officer, Captain St James, kept a stern eye on them as he saluted with his sword. Merriman met them; his officers round him. Most of them knew Andrews who, until his recent promotion, had been the First Lieutenant of the *Lord Stevenage.*

All of them joined Merriman in his cabin including the two marine officers and the ship's master, Mr Henderson.

"Right, gentlemen, Peters has refreshment ready for us," said Merriman. All began to settle in the great cabin, each accepting a glass of wine, except for Stewart who Merriman noticed still drank only water, served by Peters with the help of Merriman's clerk, Tomkins. He began, "As you know, our first duty in South American waters is to search out and destroy any of our country's enemies we can, Spanish or French, as our shipping has been repeatedly attacked here. But that is not all, gentlemen. We are to contrive to put Mr Humphries ashore near to the Spanish town of Montevideo so that he can investigate certain rumours about privateers."

A murmur went round the cabin.

"Those of you who were with me in the Caribbean will

remember how we chased some privateer ships and caught them. Two of the main culprits, a man and his wife, killed each other but the leader of the gang was one Don Carlos Galiano, the woman's father. He escaped and disappeared but rumour has it that he is down here organising privateers to prey on shipping of any nation."

"I remember it well, sir," said Captain St James, the marine officer. "A bloody business it was too. They murdered anyone who got in their way including those two thieves and murderers whom you knew and who had escaped from England."

"Quite right, Edward. We must try and catch him but it is certain to be difficult. Most of you will remember the nocturnal events during our recent voyages when we put Mr Grahame ashore to find out certain information. Well we have to do the same for Mr Humphries. Now we don't have any maps or reliable charts of the place so quite how we do it I'm not sure. It may be too far for our boats to row so perhaps we can capture a fishing boat and use that. We can all think about it and we can discuss it nearer the time."

The men nodded their assent.

"There is another important matter, gentlemen. Of course you all know that our main orders are for us to go to the South Atlantic but you don't know what else we are to do there. We are ordered to find a wrecked ship aboard which are some important documents. Mr Humphries has at last come from behind his cloak of secrecy and told me something about it. Mr Humphries, please tell my officers what you told me."

The Treasury man began, "Gentlemen this is a most unusual mission we are on and the story starts some two years ago." He then proceeded to relate the full story to them but with no mention of the precious gems in the chest they had to find.

There was silence for a moment before Midshipman Small said solemnly, "It's a big coast to search for a wreck, sir, especially if it is inland and overgrown."

Immediately and inevitably all the men tried to talk at once until Merriman rapped on the table and called for silence. "It won't be easy; we don't know how far inland the wreck lies or what condition it will be in after two years in the forest. Mr Andrews, have you any comments or questions?"

"Yes, sir, the coast of South America is a big place as Mr Small says, it could take months if not years to find the wreck. According to the story the ship was carried inland so it is unlikely that we could see it from the sea and also it could be covered with tropical growth."

Mr Humphries interjected, "We do have one more piece of information which I have kept to myself. Mr Chalmers said that they managed to take a sighting after the gales ceased and he swears that the ship was close to ten degrees of latitude south. So perhaps we could approach the shore on that line?" he said hopefully.

"What do you think, Mr Henderson?" Merriman asked the Master.

"Well, sir. That sighting could be incorrect and if it was out by only one or two degrees it would leave us a lot of coast to search. And," he added, "I have no new or reliable charts of that area. The Admiralty charts are rather vague and undetailed."

Chapter Four

The Strange Sail

At a signal from Merriman, Peters refreshed their glasses. Then Merriman continued, "There is one other matter which disturbs me. You will remember that strange sail that seemed to follow us earlier but had vanished until it reappeared this morning. Mr Humphries does not deny that it could be French or Spanish. They have spies in London and elsewhere and it is possible that our mission is not as secret as we would like it to be. Mr Humphries, would you be good enough to relate what is known about Napoleon's diplomatic approaches to England?"

"Of course, sir. You will all know that Napoleon has made suggestions that there should be a treaty between our countries. However, many people in Government and the Treasury believe this to be no more than a ruse to give him time to train more troops for his armies, organise supplies and maybe build more ships, although we aren't sure about the ships. If Mr Pitt the Prime Minister had not been forced to leave office because of ill health he would never have considered it for a moment but his successor in office, Henry Addington, seems likely to agree to it. He is a weak man, not suited to pursuing a war, but he has many supporters in the Government. So, gentlemen, we don't know what will happen next. If such a treaty is signed it will mean that France and Spain will cease to be our enemies. Until we hear otherwise though, we should consider them to still be the enemy. Of course it is unlikely that any of their ships out here will know any more than we do."

"Thank you, sir," Merriman said. "It is likely is it not, that such a treaty may lead to England having to return to France and Spain many of the Caribbean islands we took with so much bloodshed?"

"Indeed so. So, until we know what the results are in London, we must still be on our guard."

"That is true. Gentlemen, we must trust nobody. Return to your ships and your duties. Captain Andrews, will you stay behind please?"

When the cabin was cleared, Merriman said, "David, I am still wary of the ship following us so, when darkness has fallen, you will take your ship back in a wide circle in the hope that you can find him ahead of you at first light. If it is a small ship you will try to catch her but if there are any warships you must come back to us with a warning."

"Aye-aye, sir. I have been thinking about that myself," said Andrews before he left.

The following day dawned; the sun began to creep up over the horizon and then climbed rapidly higher. As it did so, the suffocating heat rose with it. Awnings rigged over the deck to give some shade did little to help and neither did wind sails rigged to direct wind below decks. Some of the men were badly sunburned in spite of warnings by Mr McBride the doctor to keep their shirts on.

Merriman was eating, if not enjoying, his meagre breakfast and thinking about his wife, the dark-haired Helen, and their two children. He wondered what problems might arise with him not there to deal with them. That led him on to thinking about his recent sponsor, Lord Stevenage, who had died and left his entire estate to Merriman. This comprised a big country estate and a town house in London, together with a large sum of money in a London bank. Problems could arise anywhere but each place had reliable servants and people in charge so there was no more to be done about it.

Helen was currently in Merriman's own estate in Cheshire, a large house overlooking the estuary of the River Dee, and she had a stern and dependable bailiff to run the estate and farms. And there was his younger brother, Matthew, who was an ensign in the 22nd Regiment of Foot, the Cheshire Regiment. His captain was married to Merriman's sister, Emily, now Mrs Saville, but Merriman had heard nothing from them for at least two years and wondered where they were.

He was still thinking about his family when, through the open skylight, he heard the lookout's hail from aloft of, "Sail astern, sir. It's *The Eagle,* sir, coming up fast."

Merriman made himself continue with his meal knowing that he would be informed, and sure enough the clatter of shoes outside the cabin and the marine sentry's call, "Mr Midshipman Evans to see you, sir," gave him some satisfaction. The boy almost tumbled into the cabin and excitedly gasped out his message that the corvette had been sighted.

"Mr Evans, you will control your excitement. You know how a report should be made, now start again and do it properly this time," said Merriman with a frown.

"Aye-aye, sir," gulped the small midshipman, more frightened by the frown than anything else. "Mr Shrigley's compliments, sir, sail has been sighted astern believed to be *The Eagle,* sir."

"Very good, Mr Evans. Don't let me have to tell you again. Now, my compliments to Lieutenant Shrigley and tell him that I will be on deck when I have finished my breakfast."

The boy fled, no doubt to tell his cronies about the imperturbable captain's refusal to be hurried over his meal.

The ship was undoubtedly *Eagle* and as it overhauled the frigate Merriman ordered both other ships to be hove to and a signal flown for the captains to come aboard and report. He also called for Humphries to join them. Andrew's report was given quietly but was a bit disturbing.

"I did as ordered, sir. I made a big circle to come up astern of that odd ship but I made the circle too big and thought I had missed her. But I found her eventually. She is a sloop sailing together with a seventy four gun ship, both of them sailing due west, sir. I think that both may have been following you until they saw my topsails and changed course. I decided not to follow them but to come and warn you of the enemy frigate."

"Interesting, very interesting, David. Do you know if they were French or Spanish ships?"

"Not for certain, sir. They were flying no flags that we could

19

see, but I thought that the frigate had the look of a Spanish ship, although I could not be certain. Perhaps they are privateers, sir."

"That is also a possibility, sir," said Stewart. "We may find out eventually but there are many Spanish towns and ports on the northern coasts of South America and in the Caribbean which harbour privateers and Spanish Navy ships so they may have been going to one of them. Meanwhile, with your agreement, sir, I think we should proceed southwards as planned. If they are following us, dawn may show the smaller ship's sails again or even the frigate if they realise that they have been discovered. There would then be no reason to hide."

Mr Humphries said, "If we do see them again, sir, I think it is obvious that they are following us. If they are it may be because of the other part of our mission of which I have not told you all the details. Spies in England may have told them."

Merriman frowned and paced up and down the limited space in the cabin whilst he considered the options. Finally he decided. "Gentlemen, this is what we will do. An hour before first light tomorrow we will reverse our course so that we may find them close enough at dawn to see what they are. We will be cleared for action, but quietly, no drums or shouting, mark you. If they are near we don't want them to hear us before we can surprise them. I want you, David, to keep to my larboard and you, Lieutenant, begin to move well out to seaward with *The Mayfly* but within signalling distance to warn us if they are passing us. But you will not engage with any warship, it is not for a brig to face up to a frigate. Do you both understand what you have to do?"

"Aye-aye, sir," they replied together, both seeming excited at the prospect of action.

Although Merriman knew that Andrews was completely reliable and would know what to do if action was joined, he still had his doubts about Stewart who had seen no action before. "Very well, gentlemen. Return to your ships, and hope for good luck tomorrow."

Chapter Five

The Great Gale

Dawn broke and, even in the pale light, they could see that nothing interrupted the horizon in any direction. The flotilla had turned as arranged, all ready for action, but it seemed to be a futile exercise. Merriman had signalled to the other ships to return to their previous course.

Until now, they had been blessed with good weather and fair winds but Merriman could see that things were about to change. Black clouds were boiling up over the horizon to the east and obscuring the sun. The wind was getting stronger and flashes of lightning could be seen in the clouds. There was to be no doubt about it, they were in for some very severe weather.

"Mr Merryweather," he called, "call all hands, this is going to be rough. I'll have the upper tops'ls off her and courses and tops'ls clewed up and reefed hard down. Have chain slings on the yards and all the guns secured with extra lashings, you know what to do."

Merryweather shouted orders and immediately there was frenzied activity. The bos'n and the topmen were aloft furling the upper tops'ls and securing them with extra lashings while others fastened the chain slings to prevent any yards falling if they broke loose. The gun captains were busy with the guns. If one broke loose it could create disaster rolling about the deck. Men could be killed and other damage done. The galley fire was doused and anything moveable tied down. Peters appeared with Merriman's bad weather coat and sou'wester just in time as he secured himself to the windward side mizzen shrouds.

Merriman could see that the other two ships had done the same with preparations only just completed before the gale was upon them. Wind began to shriek through the rigging and rain came down in torrents, near flooding the decks and gurgling out of the scuppers. The *Lord Stevenage* heeled right over to starboard under the onslaught before steadying herself as Merriman bawled, "Bear away". The ship came more upright under the skilled handling of the quartermaster and his mates at the wheel and men easing or tightening the headsail sheets as required. Merriman couldn't see the other ships but he had to trust that both captains were good seamen and would know what to do.

The sea became a maelstrom of huge waves with the crests blown off in clouds of spray and blown spume. The waves battered the ship which creaked and groaned and shivered as if in protest at the harsh treatment as the wind shrieked and screamed through the rigging. Any orders could only be passed by shouting directly into a man's ear. Merriman, cold and wet, could only imagine what conditions were like below deck. All hatches and gratings had been covered with extra canvas and boards lashed down tightly. In spite of that, water would have found its way below and be sloshing round the men's quarters so that the off duty watch would get little rest before being called up on deck again to help with any emergency.

The men on deck, the duty watch, were trying hopelessly to keep out of the wind and water. Their cold and soaked clothing did nothing to help and most men aboard were wet and bone weary with the constant movement. Some had bleeding hands from fighting ropes and canvas due to Merriman ordering small changes of sail according to changes of the wind. Some were lucky not to have been swept overboard as they moved through the swirling water on deck, clinging desperately to the heavy lifelines as they struggled to alter the set of the sails.

The officers were no better off, all being cold and wet with no relief for any of them. Bristow was on the foredeck with several men in charge of the headsail sheets and Merriman knew that he need not worry. Bristow was a fine seaman and could be relied upon even though Merriman couldn't see him for the blown spray constantly in the air.

The storm continued through the night and the next day and

night with most men battered and bruised and several men injured by snapped ropes lashing about before they could be secured or replaced. During that second night, Merriman, still tied to the shrouds, became aware that the storm was easing. The wind still blew but with lessening ferocity and the waves were still high but of lesser height than before. He roused himself from his discomfort, almost a stupor really, and looked about him. His face and clothes were caked in salt but he could see enough to realise that his ship had survived without any serious damage and the motion was already easier.

The First Lieutenant clawed his way over, clinging to anything to keep himself upright and reported to him. "I think the worst is over, sir. All is secure and the carpenter reports only a few inches of water drained down into the bilge which the pumps will clear in next to no time. And look, sir, the sun is showing itself again, that will soon dry us out."

"Very good, Henry. She is a stout ship and has proved it." Merriman fumbled with cold fingers to unfasten the rope tying him and then almost collapsed. Merryweather managed to catch him and shouted for assistance. Peters and Matthews were there and together they guided his faltering steps below, stripped his wet clothing off and put him in his cot and covered him with blankets where he fell instantly asleep.

On deck the officers and petty officers, equally as wet and tired as the men, were trying to get them on their feet to deal with the inevitable repairs. When the men complained they were told that their captain had been on deck for two days and two nights without a break, permanently there to look after them and the ship. As the weather improved so the ropes and rigging were checked for wear and replaced if necessary, the extra hatch covers taken off to allow the foetid air below to dissipate, the galley fire was lit and they had the first proper meal for two days. Merryweather restored the regular watches and half of the men found their hammocks and collapsed into them. The ship lay hove-to, well balanced under the fore and aft sails. Merryweather ordered the main and fore lower tops'ls to be set so that the ship could clear away from the land which could be seen as a hazy outline to starboard, and then continue slowly making way on her original course.

No other ships were seen that morning and, although lookouts were aloft scouring for them, no sign of their consorts could be seen. Peters kept a watch over Merriman and when he woke up at noon there was a hot meal ready for him.

"Peters, I must know what is happening. Ask the First Lieutenant with my compliments to come down."

"Well, sir, he has been awake as long as you were and he was awake all morning too. Lieutenant Shrigley has the ship now, sir."

"Very well, I'll see him. Leave Mr Merryweather asleep."

Shrigley duly appeared announced by the marine sentry. He too looked exhausted and Merriman immediately ordered him to sit down. "Now then, Alfred, how is the ship? Is there anything I should know?"

"Well the ship is in good order, sir. Half the men are cleaning dried salt off everything, the gun deck is ready for action at any time and the carpenter has reported that the bilge is dry. The bos'n and his mates have checked everything aloft and replaced or spliced some ropes but one of the jibs split top to bottom in the night. I don't know if you heard it, sir, but the topmen quickly brought the remaining canvas down for the sailmaker to repair. It was one of the heavy weather sails, sir. Sadly we lost two men in the night, probably overboard but nobody heard or saw anything." He almost fell asleep on the chair and Merriman ordered Peters to bring him a brandy which quickly wakened him up to go back on deck.

A still tired Merriman then told Peters to fetch hot water to shave him and requested some clean dry clothes. Half an hour later he was refreshed and back on deck to see for himself what shape the ship was in. He was impressed with all that had been done. The *Lord Stevenage* looked almost new but there was no sign of the other two ships until nearly dark.

Chapter Six

First sight of the Enemy

The next morning Merriman could see for himself the effects of the gale on the two other ships. Paintwork had been scoured away in places by the sea but *Eagle* looked ready for action. *The Mayfly* had lost her main topmast but otherwise seemed to be in order so he ordered both captains over to the *Lord Stevenage* to report. Both men looked grey faced and tired but Andrews reported that his ship had suffered little damage and his men had only a few minor injuries. "The men worked like slaves, sir, to bring her back to fighting trim."

"And now Captain Stewart, how did you come to lose your topmast?"

"My fault, sir. I held on to my tops'ls too long and the ship was knocked over. We had to cut it away, sir."

"I see. Do you have a spare spar to send up to replace it?" asked Merriman.

"Yes, sir, my men are preparing it even now to send it aloft. Another two or three hours should have it done."

"Good. Now, gentlemen, I know your men must be as tired as my own men so I propose we spend the rest of the day with us hove-to to enable everything repaired if necessary and the men to have as much rest as they can, although the usual watches and lookouts must be kept keen and awake."

It was the next day before the small flotilla set off southward again with men rested and all ships ready for anything. Soon afterwards the first Lieutenant appeared on the quarterdeck and asked for a quiet word with the captain.

"Certainly, Henry, what is troubling you?" replied Merriman.

"Well, sir, as you know we lost two men in the gale, both

overboard with no chance of rescue. The problem is that one of the bos'n's mates was up on the mainmast and saw three men together on the foremast main yard. They seemed to be arguing and though he couldn't see clearly, he is certain that one drew a knife and stabbed the others and threw them overside."

"Does the mate know who it was that killed the others?"

"He thinks it was one of the new men that came aboard at Portsmouth, sir, but visibility was too bad to be certain."

"A bad business, Henry. If it was murder we must find the murderer as soon as possible and hang him, but we must be careful about it. I'll ask some of the petty officers if they know of any troubles between any of the men. Have that man who saw it come down to me later and I'll..."

He was interrupted by a hail from the lookout on the maintop shouting, "Deck there, sails dead ahead," pointing with outstretched hand.

"Belay that last order, Henry. Mr Bristow, aloft with you and tell me what you see," said Merriman to the Third Lieutenant who was standing nearby. Bristow, pausing only to grab a telescope and sling it over his shoulder, rapidly climbed aloft and settled himself by the surprised lookout.

"Six small vessels, sir, look like sloops. They may be pirates attacking two trading ships heading north and there is a frigate astern of them turning and moving slowly to the southward."

"Very good, Mr Bristow, stay there and keep me informed." He turned to First Lieutenant Merryweather and said, "Henry, we'll clear for action at once."

Merryweather shouted the orders and the well trained crew knew exactly what to do. In only minutes Merryweather was able to report, "Ship's cleared for action, sir. This time the men did it in fifteen seconds faster than their previous best."

"Well done, that shows the incentive they have at the prospect of action rather than a mere exercise. Mr Merryweather, tell the men the time and that I said well done too."

He trained his telescope ahead to where he could now see the other ships hull up on the horizon and impatiently he shouted aloft, "Mr Bristow, what do you see now?"

"I can see the smaller ships clustered round the traders and I can see men fighting, sir."

Merriman immediately decided what to do. The *Lord Stevenage* was making good headway with a good wind behind her but could do better. "Mr Merryweather, I'll have the main courses loosed but keep the men up there ready to furl them again."

As usual the lower sails had been brailed up because of the possibility of fire. Merriman turned to look at the other two ships under his command. He had sent no signals to either of them but he could see that *Eagle* was ready for action and also letting her courses free. Captain Andrews knew what to do without orders but *The Mayfly* was slower to react, only just starting to brail up her courses for action. *Damn that man Stewart. He is as bad as ever. What can I do with him?* thought Merriman.

By now the flotilla was much closer to the other ships, some of which seemed to be breaking away from the rest, so Merriman shouted to the gun captain at one of the two twenty-four pounder cannon on the foredeck. Those big guns were unusual on the foredeck of a frigate but had been there since he was given command. "O'Brian, see if you can hit one of those privateers for me."

"Aye-aye, sir," replied the man with a grin and a wave of his hand.

Almost immediately the gun fired and even through the smoke Merriman could see that the heavy ball hit the privateer at the stern and shattered her rudder and sternpost.

"Well done, O'Brian. Try again on another."

This time both big guns fired as one and hit another privateer, this time amidships as it tried to turn away and flee from the action. Merriman watched in fascination as its mainmast collapsed, the ship listed and immediately began to sink.

Eagle was almost abreast of *Lord Stevenage* with Andrews watching closely, so Merriman waved to him and pointed to the four remaining privateers. Andrews responded with a wave and ordered that every sail possible was to be set. The ship surged ahead as Merriman ordered his own courses to be brailed up again. "Mr Merryweather, have Mr Bristow come down and then prepare our boarding parties."

"Aye-aye, sir."

"Mr Henderson," Merriman shouted to the Master by the ship's wheel, "bring us alongside one of those two privateers."

The two ships mentioned were in confusion, some men still fighting aboard one of the traders and others desperately trying to cast off and escape. As his ship crashed alongside one of the ships - the biggest - he saw the simpleton Biggins swinging his cutlass over his head and screaming curses at the enemy. "Bastard French buggers, I'll kill you all, just let me at 'em." The poor man thought every enemy was a Frenchman, his mind doubtless addled by the livid scar on the side of his head from an old wound occasioned in a previous encounter with the French, but he was a doughty fighter who had saved Merriman's life on occasion. The crew looked after him and his duties to make sure he didn't get into trouble and treated him almost like a mascot.

Merriman glimpsed *The Mayfly* getting alongside another privateer but there was no time to see more as, at the head of his own boarding party, he dropped onto the smaller ship's deck as Lieutenant De Mowbray led his own party, sword in hand, across for'ard. Then it was slash and slash again with his sword, cut and parry and thrust and thrust again through a man's throat or his stomach, trying to stay on his feet on the blood slippery deck and step over men either dead or writhing in agony. Merriman's foot slipped on the blood and immediately the man facing him raised his cutlass for a killing blow with a yell of triumph and a grin on his face. The grin disappeared as the Marine Captain's sword pierced his throat and he collapsed with blood pouring from his mouth and the yell became no more than a gurgle.

Merriman was conscious of his cox'n, Matthews, fighting on his left and Marine Captain St James on his right with his marines and wondered how any enemy could get to him with those two doughty fighters alongside him. Then it was up onto the trader where fighting was still going on. De Mowbray was there with him, his trouser legs and shirt splashed with blood as were Merriman's own. The men from the privateer were trying to stop them but they were still fighting the trader's crew as well and they soon called for quarter and dropped their weapons. The second privateer had managed to cast off the ropes securing it to the trader and was moving away, with the men rapidly hoisting its sails.

"Have your men round these privateers up, Mr De Mowbray, and Captain, have your marines guard them with their fixed bayonets."

"Aye-aye, sir," they both responded and Merriman was at last able to speak with men of the trader's crew.

"Where is your Captain?" he asked.

"I'm here, sir," said a man sitting on the deck leaking blood from several wounds. "May the Blessed Virgin Mary thank you for coming to our rescue. We thought we were all finished," he said, falling sideways in a faint.

"Matthews, call for Mr McBride to come over as soon as he can to tend to the Captain and the other poor fellows," said Merriman. "Now I must see what our other two ships have done."

The brig had engaged two small six gun privateer sloops and damaged one, leaving it in a sinking condition, but the other fled leaving the Portuguese trader sinking. Stewart was alongside the trader to rescue the survivors but he left the privateers to look after themselves. Then he headed back to the two sloops hit by *Lord Stevenage* which were sinking, one with no rudder and one with no mast, and fired two broadsides into them from his small six-pounder cannon to finish them off.

Meanwhile *Eagle* had caught up with the frigate which, although she had all sail set, was slow in the water. She fired a feeble and ragged broadside as *Eagle* drew alongside but it did little damage whilst the reply from *Eagle* smashed into the side, killing several men and upturning two cannon. Merriman could see Andrews' ship crash alongside the frigate and fire another broadside into her before his boarding parties climbed aboard.

He had no doubt of the result.

The captain of the surviving trader was below under the care of Doctor McBride and, as only one officer and a few crewmen had survived, and as the trader did not seem to be damaged, Merriman left Lieutenant De Mowbray and some of his boarding party to help them to clean up the mess and prepare to set sail again. The privateer that Merriman had boarded was heaped with corpses and he ordered that they should be thrown overboard. He wondered if he was becoming too harsh but he justified his decision. They were pirates after all and deserved no consideration. He instructed Lieutenant De Mowbray, with a midshipman and a small prize crew, to take command of the ship and the ten pirates who had surrendered.

Merriman shouted to Lieutenant Stewart to follow him and, as they passed the sinking trader, it rolled over and disappeared from view. Of the small sloop there was nothing to be seen except for some pieces of floating timber with a few men clinging to them. Merriman was in no mood for sympathy. The men were no better than pirates but he relented enough to have a boat put into the water to rescue them. Climbing aboard the frigate named *El Ray* or something - the paint had mostly worn away - Merriman found a jubilant Andrews waiting to report, a sullen faced man with standing next to him wearing a torn and dirty Spanish captain's uniform.

"We had only a little difficulty, sir. This is a Spanish ship and this is Captain Almeida who surrendered to us. We lost only one man dead and six with minor wounds. It was strange, sir, many of the crew seemed reluctant to fight. Those that did were quickly disposed of," and he pointed to a small heap of corpses. "The rest of them are locked below with marines on guard."

"Well done, Captain, well done. Now then, Captain Almeida, what have you to say?"

Almeida, who seemed to have a good command of English, replied, "If my ship had been in the condition she was when we left Spain three years ago, I might have beaten you. My ship is slow, coated with growth of weed below and not careened since we came out here. Beside that the hull is nearly eaten away by teredo worm. We were hoping to get back to Buenos Aires before she sank under us."

He went on to tell of poor discipline – most of the men from the original crew had died or been killed and had been replaced by untrained men, including many local natives, slaves really, who were reluctant to serve or fight, so that he had far less than half the men needed for a full crew. He looked at Merriman's blood-splashed clothing and asked, "Are you really the man in command of your three ships?"

"Indeed I am, sir, but I have had no time to change into my uniform. How many of your officers have survived, sir?"

The man replied, "Only three real Spanish officers, sir. Most of them died and were replaced by men from Buenos Aires and Montevideo, not real seamen."

"Have the Captain and the other three officers sent over to *Lord Stevenage* under guard, David. If this ship is as bad as the Captain tells us it may be of no use to us but I'll send the bos'n and his mates with the gunner and carpenter to examine her below. I don't think that you will have enough men to make a full prize crew if we keep her so I can send some over to you. Meanwhile, carry on."

He returned to his own frigate with the four Spanish officers sitting in the bows of the boat guarded by marines. On board he said to Lieutenant Bristow, "Have these Spanish officers given somewhere to clean themselves up and keep them well guarded. I will speak to Captain Almeida in my cabin when I have washed and changed. Send Mr Brockle and his mates and Mr Green and the gunner over to the prize to report on its condition."

"Aye-aye, sir," Bristow replied and turned to give the orders.

Merriman saw Doctor McBride hovering nearby so he asked, "How bad is it, Mr McBride?"

"Not too bad, sir. Of our own there is one man dead and eight wounded but only slightly. I attended to the survivors of the trader's crew but I brought the captain back here so that I could keep an eye on him. His name is Marco Macleod, sir, he is weak but will recover and wants to see you."

"Very good, I'll see him later when I am cleaned up."

Chapter Seven

The Captives Questioned

An hour later, clean and wearing his usual seagoing clothing, Merriman was pacing up and down in his great cabin, tugging at his ear as was his habit when considering a problem. This time he needed to decide what to do with all the prisoners and the survivors from the two trading ships. His thinking was interrupted by the marine sentry thumping his musket on the deck and announcing that Lieutenant Stewart was aboard and wanting to see him.

"Very well, send him in," replied Merriman, more than a little annoyed at having his thoughts interrupted.

Stewart entered. "I'm sorry to disturb you, sir, but I thought I should make my report at once."

"Yes, Mr Stewart, what have you to report?"

"We sank one of the privateers and rescued an officer and three of the crew from the trader, sir. The rest had been killed. The pirates had set a charge to explode when they left but I was able to save an officer and three crew from the ship before it went down. The captain was dead, sir."

"I saw that you left the men from the privateer to drown, Mr Stewart. Prisoners could reveal valuable information, remember that. But I must add, I was going to leave them but you will have seen that I had them picked up, there were only three of them left. Had you any casualties on your ship?"

"Only two men slightly wounded, sir, but they will be alright. I saw that you saved the other trader, sir, and captured the frigate. Some nice prize money for us all, I think, sir."

"Then you can think again, Mr Stewart. That ship is in a very bad state and may not float much longer. I have sent men over to inspect it." Merriman paused as the marine sentry called out that the bos'n, carpenter and gunner were outside to report.

Send them in, if you please," replied Merriman. "Mr Stewart, you might as well stay and hear this."

The three men entered and stood in front of Merriman's table. The carpenter, Mr Green, spoke first. "Sir, that ship is in a terrible bad state, sir. The timbers below water level are as rotten as they can be. I could almost push my finger through. She needs a long time in a good dockyard to make her fit for sea again."

"As bad as that, is it? And what say you, Mr Brockle, what of the stores aboard?"

"Mostly rotten cordage. The spare sails are mildewed and rotten. I wouldn't want to use any of it on our ship, sir."

Mr Salmon the gunner spoke next. "The guns are old and mostly worn out and useless, sir, though there is some powder and shot we could use. Not much else worth saving, sir."

"Did any of you check the food and water aboard?" asked Merriman.

"One of me mates did, sir. There is only a bit of food not fit to eat and the water casks are mostly empty, although the casks themselves are good enough for us to use. They'll need a good scouring first, sir. In the hold we found rolls and bundles of expensive looking cloth and boxes and boxes of silver items. At least we think it is silver, sir, it's all tarnished and dirty."

"Thank you, gentlemen. I will tell you later what my orders are."

"Aye-aye, sir," they chorused together and left.

"So you see, Mr Stewart, it is a prize not worth keeping. Now back to your ship, fresh orders will follow."

When the man had gone, Merriman went up on deck and began pacing up and down the quarterdeck, continuing to tug at his ear while he considered the options. First, the frigate was no use and would have to be sunk after anything worth having had been taken out of her. Then there were the prisoners and survivors to consider. The ghost of an idea was beginning to form in his mind about future plans. *Perhaps they could, no, simply too far-fetched, and yet?* He continued to pace whilst tugging at his ear and with a scowl set upon his face.

He became aware of the Spanish captain, Almeida, approaching as if wishing to speak with him and was equally aware of his own men busy removing the man. They knew well enough that their captain was not to be approached in such a way when he was deep in thought. His habit of ear tugging was well known to all his crew.

Merriman paced and thought some more. Finally he asked the duty midshipman to call the doctor up on deck.

"Ah, Mr McBride, how are your patients and in particular how is Captain Macleod?"

"They are all recovering well, sir. The captain is weak but will survive. He is though desperate to speak to you."

"Very well, I'll go below and see him right away."

The doctor led the way to his own small cabin where a heavily bandaged Macleod was lying in the doctor's own cot with his eyes closed. Merriman coughed and, when the wounded man opened his eyes, he said, "The doctor tells me that you will recover, sir, though you are very weak from loss of blood."

"Yes, senor, I'm as feeble as little cat, but I must know about my ship and crew. Senor, I implore you, what can you tell me?"

"Your ship is safe, sir, with little damage, but I'm sorry to have to tell you that many of your crew were lost. There is only one officer and four men left alive. I have put some of my men aboard to help them until we have decided what to do."

"My men fought well, Captain, but we would have lost if your ship had not appeared. We had been far off shore and out of danger as we had thought when those privateers, pirates really, caught us. But what of the other ship that was with us?"

"Sunk and lost, Captain. The captain was killed and only four of her men survived. They are safe aboard one of my ships."

The man groaned and shut his eyes. "That other captain was my brother," he said.

"I'm sorry, Captain," said Merriman. "I'll leave you now while I decide what we can do with our prisoners."

He returned to the great cabin but it took him only a few minutes to finalise his plan and so he then called his available officers Merriman, Bristow and the marine captain St James to join him.

"Gentlemen, this is what we must do. The frigate is in too bad a condition to keep as a prize as she is already close to sinking, so we'll have everything off her that will be useful to us, the good water casks and such. That will include the silver and rolls of cloth if they are fit to use and I have an idea that the sails on her yards are the best they have, so we'll have those too. Then we'll sink her. The men we saved off the sunken Portuguese trader can join their friends aboard the other one we saved. They should be enough to sail her to a suitable port. The main problem is all our prisoners. We have twenty Spanish including Captain Almeida and perhaps thirty of the native people who were forced to join them. And then we have thirteen or fourteen survivors off the privateer pirate ships including some Spanish there too. I have my own ideas but I would like to hear your own thoughts on the matter."

"Well, sir, the Spanish captain and men are, I suppose, legitimate prisoners of war and should be treated accordingly," said Merryweather, "but the privateers are different. If they have a Letter of Marque from a Spanish government we can't execute them but otherwise they are pirates and we can legally hang them, although the native men off the frigate are again different."

"All that is so, Henry, but the frigate was in company with the pirates and could with certainty can be classed as one of them," said Merriman. "Do you have any ideas, Eric?"

"Well no, sir," replied Lieutenant Bristow. "Except that if the Spanish were pirates too, then they could not be classed as prisoners of war and we should hang them, although I believe that slavery is still practised in Portuguese colonies and that might be one way to deal with them."

"In favour of slavery are you, Eric? Don't forget that most of our possessions in the Caribbean are still worked by slaves although there is a strong move in Parliament to do away with it."

The man frowned.

"Well then, we will leave that for the moment until I have

spoken to the two captains we have aboard. In the meanwhile, make arrangements for all the Portuguese seamen to join their fellows on the trader that has survived. Send boats over to *Eagle* to tell Captain Andrews what I have decided. He is to keep half of the prisoners under guard and send the others over here to be kept under guard below. You can look after all that, Captain St James. Further, ask him with my compliments to take out of that ship anything that we can use and then we will sink it. Send all our boats over and the bos'n, carpenter and gunner as well, they already know what they want. Make certain that the hands don't get their hands on any rum, brandy or wine that may be there. And I want most of that to be done before dark, if possible. Now, Mr Merryweather, I'll have that Spanish captain in here with a marine guard."

A little while later the sentry knocked and announced, "Prisoner and escort here, sir." The Captain and two marines entered and it was obvious that the man had worked himself into a rage because he began to swear and shout almost before he was fully into the cabin. Merriman ignored him and merely signalled to one of the marines who clamped a big horny hand over the man's mouth. When the man had stopped trying to shout, Merriman said mildly, "Captain Almeida, you are supposed to be an officer and a gentleman, I think, and you should behave like one. Now if you can control your temper you will be allowed to speak, quietly. Is that understood?"

The man nodded and the marines released him. Merriman pointed to a chair and the man sat down. "Now then, Captain, what do you wish to say?" said Merriman.

"I must protest, sir, at the treatment of myself and my officers. Our countries are at war and we must be treated as prisoners of war."

Merriman leaned back in his chair and regarded the Spaniard with a baleful stare. "We found you sailing in the company of pirates, sir. Why should you not be treated as such? Have you a Letter of Marque from your government?" The man shook his head but Merriman held up his hand before the Spaniard could reply "We captured your ship, which we consider to be a legitimate prize, but we shall sink it in the morning as it is too rotten to be of any use. We also found certain items of expensive cloth and boxes of silver amongst other stuff. I think that is booty, the proceeds of robbery. What do you say to that, Captain Almeida?"

As Merriman was speaking the wretched man seemed to shrivel in his chair but made an effort to answer. "The boxes of silver, sir, are intended for Spain if I can get it there. The cloth we took from an Indiaman in the south Atlantic weeks ago to be taken to Buenos Aires. That was a prize of war and legally taken."

"And what did you do with the crew?" asked Merriman in a deceptively mild voice.

"Most of them were killed, the rest we set adrift in boats with water and some biscuits to take their chances. We were not far from land, sir," answered Almeida.

"I see, well I tell you I don't believe any of your lies. If legally obtained, the silver would undoubtedly have been melted down into ingots to make it easier to transport to Spain. The other stuff is so mixed up and dirty, I believe, as I said before, that it is the proceeds of theft and piracy. Nor do I believe that you saved any of the Indiaman's crew. I think you killed them all and you should be hanged as a common pirate."

Almeida drew himself up and said proudly, "I am an officer of His Most Catholic Majesty's Navy. If you hang me or any of my men that is a far more despicable crime than piracy which we were forced into to survive."

Merriman studied him a while before he said to one of the marines, "Sergeant, take this man below with the others and put him in chains like a common felon."

Chapter Eight

Captured Frigate Sent to the Bottom

It was nearly full dark before Merriman's weary officers reported that almost all of his orders had been completed. The useful contents of the frigate had been taken out to be shared between the three ships of the flotilla according to their needs. That included the powder and shot for the guns, water barrels and a collection of small arms, swords, pistols and muskets with plenty of powder and shot for those. Lanterns and oil had been taken as had a multiplicity of small items including tobacco. There were several spars that could be of use but they had been left to be floated over in daylight, and there were three seaworthy ship's boats and the ship's sails had been furled ready to bring across.

Dawn found the three ships of Merriman's flotilla all at action stations as usual. With no enemy revealed in the growing light, orders were given to secure the guns and to return to normal duties. After their breakfast, men were soon busy, cleaning the decks, washing and polishing and stowing most of the stuff taken from the Spanish frigate. Boats from all three ships were busy carrying goods between them and the spare spars were floated over to *Lord Stevenage* ready to be lifted aboard.

Merriman watched all this activity from the quarterdeck while he took his usual exercise walking up and down. He became aware that petty officers were reporting to the officers and they were all standing expectantly ready to report to him. The first lieutenant was the first one to approach him. "Sir, all has been done as you ordered but there is still the question of what we will do with that rotten frigate."

"Thank you, Mr Merryweather, we shall sink it. Are you sure

that there is nothing left aboard that could be of use to us?"

"Yes, sir, nothing that isn't rotten, mildewed or otherwise unserviceable."

"Good, now have the gunner rig charges in the hold with fuses timed to blow up as one. Set them half an hour to give him and his men time to get clear and have the marines bring the Spanish captain and his officers to me here."

With a quick, "Aye-aye Sir," the lieutenant began to pass the necessary orders. A boat pushed off with the gunner and his mates aboard along with three small kegs of gunpowder and a coil of slow match. The midshipman in command, Mr Evans, brought the boat smartly alongside the frigate and then waited for the destruction party to complete their work and return to the boat. Once they were aboard, the crew rowed hard to get as far away as possible before the charges went off.

Merriman turned to the young midshipman standing near to him and said, "Mr Green, be so good as to go below and ask Mr McBride if Captain Macleod is well enough to be brought on deck. He may like to see what is going to happen."

"Aye-aye, sir," said the boy and he disappeared below. Meanwhile the Spanish officers had been brought on deck, still in chains and lined up on the side deck. Two of McBride's assistants struggled up the companionway with Captain Macleod sitting in a chair. They put him down on the quarterdeck, McBride keeping a careful eye on him.

"Captain, I hope you are feeling better. The doctor is very good at what he does," said Merriman.

"Oh yes, sir. Your men told me what is going to happen. I wouldn't miss it for the world."

"Good. May I ask you how it is that a Portuguese captain can speak such good English?"

"Well, sir, my father was a Scotsman who settled down here and married my mother. They both insisted that I spoke their own language perfectly."

"Excellent, Captain. I would like to have a long chat with you when you feel well enough." Merriman then approached the group of bewildered Spanish officers. "I have brought you on deck, Captain Almeida, so that you may see the end of your ship. Every captain should see that."

At that moment the boat returned alongside and the gunner approached. "All done as ordered, sir," he reported, knuckling his forehead. "Should only be a few minutes more."

"Well done, Mr Salmon," said Merriman.

As it happened there was a pause of only two or three minutes before three distinct rumbles like that of thunder, were heard and the ship began to settle. "Those charges should have taken the bottom out of her, sir," said Salmon.

Indeed the frigate was sinking more rapidly as the sea poured in but was still on an even keel. Soon the water was rising above the gundeck and then the quarterdeck and then the hull disappeared with only the masts still showing. As the mainmast finally disappeared, Almeida drew himself up as high as his chains allowed and raised his hat in salute. Merriman noticed that tears were running down his cheeks as he did so. "Sergeant, you may take these men below again," he said. "Captain Almeida, I'll speak to you later."

Back on his quarterdeck Merriman spoke to Captain Macleod. "Captain, do you feel up to being taken to my cabin? I would like to find out more from you about conditions here off the coast of Brazil and what you know of Spanish activities here."

"Indeed, sir, I am more than willing," Macleod replied.

"Good man. Doctor, I think you should come down too to keep an eye on your patient, and Mr Humphries would you come too?"

Down in the great cabin, Macleod was soon comfortably installed in a chair with a welcome glass of claret in his hand and Merriman began. "Captain, my friend here, Mr Humphries is a representative of our government. We have been sent here to find out more about the Spanish and privateer activities along the coasts. Many of our trading vessels have disappeared in these waters. Captain, where were you and your brother sailing to and what was your cargo?"

"My brother Jorge and myself worked together in a little

trading venture with just two small ships. We were making a good living and hoped to buy another ship to join us, but with my brother dead that is not likely to happen," he said with a catch in his voice. He took another sip of claret and continued, "Generally we trade up and down this coast, sir. Spain and Portugal are not at war – *yet,* "he added significantly, "although there have been several skirmishes on the southern border between ourselves and the Spanish, so we trade between the Spanish towns of Buenos Aires and Montevideo and our own towns of Salvador, Rio de Janeiro, Sao Paulo and other villages. Everything needed has to be taken by ship as there is too much jungle and swamp inland with virtually no roads. We were sailing north to Salvador when we were attacked so you must have passed there."

Merriman nodded and Macleod continued, "We carry fresh but salted meat and also hides and other cattle products as well as the deep blue dye called indigo from the Spanish towns and take sugar, rum and Brazilwood there and occasionally some gold and diamonds from the hills and mountains to pay for it. It has been profitable until now," he said sadly. "I don't know why our ships should have been attacked, sir, we are carrying only meat and hides, as is well known. Perhaps the pirates thought we had more."

"No doubt, Captain, no doubt. Now tell me what is Brazilwood, I have not heard of it before."

"It used to be one of our main trading products in the last century but it is much reduced now. It produces dyes in shades of deep reds and purples, but is not much used anymore."

"I see. Now you tell me that you were going to the town of Salvador, perhaps you could advise me if it is a good place for my ships to go to replenish with water, fruit, vegetables and of course meat. Naturally we will pay for everything in gold."

"Yes, we were sailing for Salvador. A lot of meat is needed in the towns and villages along here, to feed the slaves you see. If you will follow me I can take you to a snug harbour where you can get everything you need."

"Slaves, eh!" said Merriman with distaste. "I thought that

trade was beginning to be stamped out. I know that English plantations in the Caribbean islands still use slaves but there is a strong movement in our Parliament to make it illegal."

"None the less, sir, it is still very active in Brazil and I am sure that it will be for many years to come."

"And is this town of Salvador suitable for replenishing everything we need for three ships, Captain Macleod?"

"Oh yes indeed, sir. It isn't just a town, it is a fine city with a good harbour and until only a few years ago it was the capital of this country, after all, we Portuguese have been here since the sixteenth century. The city is on a peninsula called Bahia which protects the town and harbour from Atlantic gales."

At this point Mr Humphries, who had been silent so far, said, "I look forward to seeing your city, sir. I know it has some fine buildings and a magnificent cathedral and has expanded a lot in the last century, but I have never been there. My knowledge of it is all second hand from people who have visited."

"I'm sure you'll be impressed, sir. I would be happy to show you round," answered Macleod.

Chapter Nine

Salvador

On a near perfect tropical morning, the *Lord Stevenage* and the two other ships of the small flotilla, followed by the captive pirate ship manned by a small prize crew under Lieutenant De Mowbray, sailed in to the anchorage and harbour of Salvador. The *Lord Stevenage* fired the customary salute of a broadside with each cannon firing one after the other from for'ard to aft and the gunner Mr Salmon counting the timing, "Number one gun, fire, if I wasn't a fool I wouldn't be here. Number two gun, fire, I don't know why I bother. Number three gun, fire," and so on, continuing the litany until the salute was completed. The big stone fort on the headland fired a salute in return and in the sudden silence the frightened seabirds settled back on to the rocks and sea.

The sky was an almost impossible blue and there was a gentle breeze to help the ships to come to anchor. The only thing wrong with the day was the heat from the sun which, even so early, was almost too much to bear beating though the awnings which had been rigged over the decks.

Captain Macleod had explained that there was a governor in residence and now said, "That is the Fort Santa Antonia which was built about two hundred years ago, Captain Merriman, but you will have noticed many other forts along the coast, I'm sure. Salvador is well protected."

Merriman studied the forts and the harbour with a keen eye. "Tell me, Captain, do you get many Spanish vessels in here?"

"Yes we do, sir. As we are not at war with Spain or France it is mostly trading ships and only rarely do we see warships. Trade is the life blood of this country so that, as long as the Spanish behave themselves, we will trade with them. Of course the sailors want to visit the brothels and taverns in that rough area over there so we keep a watch on them. If they stray into the better parts of the city, the army sends them packing. So, Captain, may I invite you and your fellow captains ashore? You will have to meet the governor and other notable gentlemen and I would be pleased to take you to my home."

"Thank you, sir, we would be honoured, but first I must invite Captains Andrews and Stewart to join us here with Mr Humphries and then we shall go ashore together."

And so, wearing their best uniforms and with the boat's crew smartly dressed in blue striped trousers and blue shirts provided for them from Merriman's own pocket, the five of them were rowed to some wet stone steps which they climbed up to the top of the jetty. Merriman instructed his cox'n Matthews to pull back to the ship but keep a lookout for their return. "Better that than sitting in the boat in the full sun, eh, Matthews?"

"Aye-aye, sir, thank you," the man replied gratefully.

A small crowd had gathered and a well-dressed woman hastened forward to greet Captain Macleod with a warm embrace. "Welcome home, my dear, I'm happy to see you again, but I see you are limping. Are you hurt?"

"I was, but thanks to these gentlemen of the Royal Navy I survived. Now we must go to see the governor and I will bring my friends to our house afterwards and tell you all about it."

Of course all the talking was in rapid Portuguese but Humphries translated.

Macleod turned to a Portuguese officer in a splendid uniform standing by a carriage who was waiting with ill-concealed impatience to be introduced to the visitors. He was accompanied by a squad of four dragoons who were not as splendidly dressed but who rode their horses with ease. That duty done and after the obligatory raising of hats and bowing the officer told them that the governor had instructed him to bring them up to his palace with the honour guard. He did not speak much English so Macleod translated.

As the party proceeded through the town they were amazed at the sight of so many beautiful houses built in obvious

Portuguese style, magnificent palaces and churches and above them all towered a magnificent cathedral. "My word, Captain, I have been in Portugal but have seen nowhere finer than this," remarked Merriman as the party entered a paved courtyard through a splendidly decorated archway. The escort of soldiers disappeared and the officer led the party up a short flight of broad stone steps, through a superbly carved doorway guarded by soldiers. Through that they entered a vast hall with a wide stairway leading up to a broad balcony which Merriman assumed led to offices and maybe bedrooms.

The officer led them to another beautifully carved door and knocked. A voice replied and the officer ushered them into a small room furnished as an office. The tall man behind the desk rose and came forward as they entered. The officer tried his best to introduce the visitors but it was obvious that he was struggling with the English language so Macleod excused himself and took over the introductions himself. "Your Excellency," he said in Portuguese, "these gentlemen are from the British Navy ships that saved my ship and no doubt my life when we were attacked by pirates."

He introduced the four of them to the governor and there was much bowing with their hats off as the governor welcomed them and called for a servant to bring refreshments. When all were seated, he turned to Captain Macleod and in rapid Portuguese he asked what had happened. Merriman and the others waited for Humphries to translate which he did, confirming that the captain had given an exact account of the events. The governor sat there getting redder and redder in the face with his rising temper until he controlled himself and spoke to Merriman. Again Merriman had to wait for a translation from Humphries who told him that Governor Gilberto Escoveda was thanking them most profusely and offering that the town could supply everything needed - at a price of course.

There was more conversation and the party left after some additional bowing to each other. Humphries whispered to Merriman that he would tell him everything once they were outside where the carriage was waiting. The officer was not there so Macleod gave the coachman some quick instructions then told them, "We are going to my house now, gentlemen, to meet my wife and family and we can have a light lunch if you are agreeable?"

The captain's house was a good size in typical Portuguese style and before they entered he asked them to make themselves comfortable whilst had a private word with his wife about the loss of his brother. He disappeared whilst a black servant took them to a large, comfortable seating area.

They sat there chatting about what they had seen, the architecture, the people and the comfort of the house until the captain returned. "I apologise for leaving you alone but I had to tell my wife about the loss of my brother, Jorge. It was difficult because he is – was, married to my wife's sister and she is taking it very hard."

Merriman was on his feet in an instant, "Captain Macleod, we should not be here on such a sad occasion. You have enough to do without worrying about us. Perhaps we can meet again tomorrow to discuss the supply of our ships?"

"That is a kind thought, Captain, thank you. The governor's coach has left but I will order mine out for you now and I will send it for you in the morning."

Chapter Ten

Replenishing in Salvador

Back aboard the *Lord Stevenage* with the others, Merriman said, "I shall need an exact list of all that your ship is short of. Obviously fruit, including the citrus fruits we have become so fond of, fresh vegetables and meat. It seems that there is plenty of salted beef and pork available but I hope we can obtain some fresh meat. I for one would welcome some fresh roast beef and ham and I know, if my memory serves me right, that many of you would love fresh pork crackling. Now back to your ships, gentlemen, I look to see you back here at the start of the forenoon watch with your lists."

When he was left alone, Merriman called his clerk Tomkins down to his cabin and told him about the need for lists of ship's requirements. Tomkins had been with him since Merriman found him begging on the steps of the Admiralty several years ago. He had been badly wounded in a sea battle years before and abandoned by the navy who only wanted whole men to man its ships. Merriman had remembered that Tomkins had saved him from a fall from aloft and so he had promised him a place in his ship. The man was physically incapable doing heavy work but had a good knowledge of writing and arithmetic and had rapidly proved himself invaluable as Merriman's clerk.

"Tomkins, you can tell the bos'n, carpenter, master, gunner and the doctor to provide their lists as soon as possible. And then pass the word, with my compliments, for Mr Merryweather and other officers to come down to see me."

The first lieutenant must have been waiting for the summons because barely a minute passed before the marine sentry knocked on the door and announced, "First lieutenant and officers to see you, sir."

Merriman told them all that had happened ashore and that they must provide their lists of requirements and that the petty officers were already working on that. "Mr Merryweather and Mr Shrigley, please stay behind for a moment when the others have left." At that broad hint everyone left the cabin and left the three of them alone.

"Now then, gentlemen, has anything happened that I should know about?" asked Merriman.

"No, sir, nothing out of the ordinary. The men spend a lot of time gazing at the town and talking about the taverns and women there. As I say, nothing out of the ordinary, sir," reported Shrigley. "All the usual shipboard jobs are being done and I believe you will find all in order."

"I don't doubt that for a minute, Alfred, but what concerns me more is what we have to do with our prisoners. By my count we have four Spanish officers and twenty four of the original crew of the frigate plus some thirty of the native people who were forced to be there. Of the privateers there are I think, only thirteen. And of course we have the captured sloop as well. Have either of you thought any more about that problem?"

The two officers shook heads in unison and Merryweather said, "Well, sir, we have discussed it briefly but can think of nothing better to do with them other than turn them over to the Portuguese, sir."

"Well, gentlemen, I have my own idea as to what should be done with them, but that can wait for now."

The following morning, Captain Macleod's own carriage arrived on the quayside to take Merriman, Humphries, Andrews and Stewart, armed with their lists, to the trader's house. Arriving at their destination they were welcomed by the Captain who met them in his hall and told the coachman to take the coach round into the shade of the stables. Glad to be out of the scorching heat, Merriman sank gratefully into a comfortable chair as did the others. A coloured servant in uniform carried drinks around which Merriman and Andrews accepted but Stewart asked for only fruit juice.

Merriman produced the lists of ships requirements and said, "Captain, here are the lists for each ship. Please tell us the best of the warehouses we should go to. Of course we can provide working parties to help carry the goods."

Macleod studied the lists, nodding his head from time to time before saying, "Gentlemen, I can supply most of the foodstuff you need including salt beef and pork in barrels. The meat was salted and packed under my supervision in Montevideo so you won't get any fresher meat unless it walks to your ships. Fruit and vegetables can be bought from outlying farms and if you have good clean water barrels and a party of men I can show you the best place to fill them. Most of the goods you need I can provide myself from my own warehouses, free of course, in gratitude for saving me and my ship."

Merriman objected. "We can't expect you to supply all that for nothing, Captain. We can pay for it."

"Yes, Captain Merriman, I know, but I wish to do so. If not for you I might well be dead and my ship and cargo lost. No, I insist. The water is there in the river for the taking if you have barrels, and I can supply the salt beef and pork and arrange for live animals for you if you want them. I have a good stock of canvas and rope but I cannot supply powder and shot. That must be purchased from the state armoury. Live chickens and eggs, geese and ducks can be bought from a very good farm not far away and I see that you have asked for brandy, rum and tobacco together with some medicines and bandages for your good Doctor McBride."

"Thank you, sir. The first thing will be fresh water, vegetables and fruit, lemons, limes and oranges if you can find them. Will you be able to provide us with horses and carts to fetch the water?"

"Of course, sir, but because of the weight bullocks would be better. You will need to bring your ships alongside the quay for loading the water and other things. There will be room for two of your ships at once. I'll send wagons and drivers to your ship right away so that your men can start to unload your water barrels directly. My men can show them where the water is.

Perhaps I should arrange for the other things on your lists be delivered to each ship in turn?"

"That will be most agreeable, sir," replied Merriman. "But I must send my officers back to my ships to give the necessary orders. Your wagons can follow to collect our barrels. Mr Stewart, I suggest you and Captain Andrews should lay your ships alongside first. Mr Humphries and I must stay here as we have much to discuss with the good captain."

"Aye-aye, sir," they replied and, as they rose, Macleod crossed to a bell pull to call a servant to send for the coach to take them back to their ships.

Settled again and with fresh drinks, Merriman said, "Captain I have a few questions about conditions out here. First, do you know a Spaniard by the name of Don Carlos Galiano?"

"Galiano? Yes, we do know that evil man. He is the one who controls the privateers or pirates in Montevideo. He has been a thorn in the side of honest traders for the last three or four years."

"That is what is suspected by our people in London, sir. Captain Merriman met him in Jamaica but he escaped before he could be captured," said Humphries. "We have been sent here to try and capture him and destroy his ships. Have you met him, Captain?"

"Not actually met him, no, but I trade with Montevideo and I have often seen him in the harbour there and I do know where he lives."

"That is interesting, Captain, and would you be able to point out his ships if you saw them?"

"Possibly, but I hear that he has many more than I have seen."

"I see, I see. Another question, can you speak the native language, sir?"

"Well, a little. All traders must but there are so many dialects that it is not easy. What do you have in mind?"

"At the moment but a few vague ideas, I need to consider it more."

"Well, sir, if you have no more questions my wife wishes to see you and we have a cold lunch prepared, so if you would follow me?"

The captain's wife was the lady who had met Macleod on the quayside. She curtseyed to Merriman as he bowed. "Dear Captain Merriman," she said, "I cannot thank you enough for saving my husband. Is there anything I can do to make your stay here more pleasant?"

"Thank you, ma'am, it was fortunate that my ships arrived in time. Your husband has done everything possible for me and my men. Pray say no more about it."

"Has he told you about your invitation to the governor's house tomorrow evening?"

"No, ma'am he hasn't," said Merriman as he looked at her husband with raised eyebrows.

"I was just getting to that, Alicia," said Macleod testily. "Well, sir, you and your officers are invited to the governor's house tomorrow evening for dinner and entertainment. Carriages will be sent for you at seven o'clock sharp."

"My word, I'm honoured, sir, thank you. We will be glad to accept and we shall have to have our best uniforms prepared."

After the meal, Merriman thanked Mrs Macleod for her hospitality and asked if a carriage could be found to take him back to his ship.

Chapter Eleven

The Governor's Banquet

Arriving back on the quayside, Merriman found both *The Eagle* and *The Mayfly* already alongside with men busy lifting water barrels out of the hold and loading them onto stout wagons. Each of these was drawn by four bullocks. Empty barrels were stacked on the quayside. Other men had been sent down to a nearby beach where they were busy scouring the inside of the barrels with sand before rinsing them out with seawater. Carts had already arrived loaded with the items requested and men swarmed over them to unload the goods and transfer them to the ships. Tackles rigged to the yardarms aided their efforts.

Captain Andrews met him on the quayside with a big grin on his face. "It's going well, sir. One load of barrels has been scoured already and has been taken to be filled. I expect them back any time now. Captain Macleod has organised it very well, sir. Each cart that arrives is listed to which ship it has to be delivered and both ships already have plenty of barrels of salted meat below. The officers and petty officers are checking everything." As he spoke two more wagons arrived, one for each of the two ships, loaded with canvas and cordage.

"There will be tobacco, rum and brandy coming, David, so have a watch out for them. You know what Jack is like if he smells rum. They'll try to break a cask open if they can, accidentally of course. And we have to make provision for livestock too on all ships, small pigs, geese, chickens and the like, so have the carpenter make pens where possible. They will make a welcome change from salt meat for us all. And you'll have to detail men to look after them but I'm sure they will be eaten before long. Now, I see that Matthews is waiting here, so Mr Humphries and I shall go back to *Lord Stevenage* to have a start made on bringing up water barrels and empty meat casks." About to turn away, Merriman recalled other matters and said, "Oh yes, we are invited to the governor's residence tomorrow night for dinner, so I think you and two of your officers and a midshipman should go. Pass the word to Captain Stewart and his officers. I want all of you to be in your best uniforms, shoes polished and, oh… you know what is required."

Back aboard his own ship, welcomed by the usual ceremony of whistles and salutes, Merriman looked round at all the activity.

"Welcome back, sir," said Lieutenant Merryweather. "I have organised the boats to start taking our casks over to the beach where they can be scoured out and, as you can see, more barrels are ready on deck to go ashore."

"Excellent work, Henry. Now tell the boat crews to leave the washed casks and barrels ashore under guard. They will be taken by the bullock carts to be filled and then left on the quayside to be loaded on our ship when we go alongside."

"Aye-aye, sir, and I have already arranged for your servants Peters and Tomkins to be ready to check everything that comes aboard. I trust that is agreeable to you, sir?"

With a nod Merriman and Humphries disappeared below, both glad to get out of the sun's heat and dispense with their heavy coats to change into something lighter. Peters was ready with a welcome drink of fruit juice and, when Merriman queried where it came from, the man said, "Sneaked ashore, sir, early, to find a market. There is one not far away, it was just opening and there is a wonderful choice of foods, some of which I haven't seen before, sir. I bought the fruit and took the liberty of buying a piglet. I thought you would enjoy some fresh roast pork, sir."

"Well done, you rogue, and where is it now?"

"It is already with the cook, sir, being prepared for your dinner tonight."

"Good, but it won't be me alone. I'll invite Mr Humphries and the two captains each with one officer and one midshipman as well as one of my officers and a midshipman to share it. That makes ten of us and I think one piglet might serve us all."

"Aye-aye, sir. I picked out really fat little beggar, sir. It will be plenty, and will you have some of the new Spanish wine just come aboard?"

"Yes, and tell the cook we want plenty of crackling."

By nightfall the two ships were nearly fully loaded and the work continued by the light of lanterns. As per Merriman's instructions, the invited officers arrived on board the *Lord Stevenage* at the appointed time. Captain Andrews brought with him his third lieutenant, James Duddy, and a scrawny midshipman by the name of James Gilmore. Captain Stewart brought his second lieutenant, Brian Lester, and one Walter Owen, midshipman. Lester was very young and seemed to be little older than Midshipman Owen, but he must have passed the exam for lieutenant at the earliest age possible. Lieutenant De Mowbray and Midshipman Evans made up the numbers with Humphries and Merriman.

Merriman welcomed them all into the great cabin where Peters and Tomkins served wine to all except Captain Stewart who was given the usual fruit juice and water. "Well now, gentlemen, I am delighted to welcome you here and I hope we may get to know each other a little better over dinner."

The roast pork duly arrived with an apple sauce and a veritable mound of vegetables. As Merriman stood up to carve the piglet, the smell of the meat was overwhelming. He saw the three young midshipmen practically drooling at the sight. Peters and Tomkins then served it out and brought to the table another dish of something which smelled good.

"What is that, Peters?" asked Merriman.

"It's a sort of seasoning, sir, recommended by the cook. He went ashore with me to the market and bought a few things."

"I see. Now, gentlemen, fall to and remember that 'Good digestion waits on appetite and health on both'. I believe that is from King Lear."

"Who is King Lear, sir?" ventured Midshipman Owen in a squeaky voice.

"Lear, young man, is one of William Shakespeare's plays. I

have read a lot of Shakespeare over the years and I recommend him to you."

"If I may, sir, I have an apt quotation," said De Mowbray. "It is 'Men sit down to that nourishment which is called supper' from Love's Labour Lost, another play of Shakespeare."

As the meal progressed, the three young midshipmen emptied their plates as fast as they could and looked around hopefully for some more which, to their delight, Peters delivered to them and also to those officers who wanted more. All were now a little red faced from the heat and the wine.

Lieutenant Lester barely concealed a belch and said, "This crackling, sir, I've not eaten better since I last ate my mother's cooking. If I may?" He reached for another piece and crunched on it.

Conversation began to flow more easily as the wine took effect and the men from the different ships began to get to know each other.

"Mr De Mowbray, John, have you read much Shakespeare then?" Merriman asked.

"Not as much as I would like to, sir, I haven't the books, but I do know something of Henry the Fifth and Francis Bacon's writings."

"Well I have copies of Hamlet, Henry the Fifth, The Merchant of Venice and Macbeth which you might like to borrow. Mr Humphries' predecessor on this ship was a keen student of Shakespeare and we had a sort of contest between us as each tried to find an apt quotation for events. I hope we may do so when you have read more."

The plates were cleared and then biscuits and cheese appeared. "I can't boast about either the biscuits or cheese, gentlemen, they are Spanish but are fresh aboard," said Peters.

At last they finished eating and their glasses were filled with brandy. Merriman looked round the table and said mildly to Lieutenant Duddy, "Would you give your midshipman a nudge, James, he is I think the youngest and should propose the Loyal Toast."

Poor Gilmore was nearly asleep, full of food and wine when

he was nudged awake by Duddy. He came to with a start and looked round bewilderedly until Duddy whispered, "The Loyal Toast now, your task."

The boy lurched to his feet, grabbed his glass and squeaked, "The King" to which all responded, standing awkwardly beneath the deckhead. "I'm sorry, sir, I fell asleep. I've not eaten so well for a long time," said a red faced and embarrassed midshipman.

"Don't worry, young man, I think we all might have done the same when we were midshipmen," said Merriman to the nods and smiles of the company. The evening passed all too rapidly and closed with all thanking Merriman for his hospitality.

At first light the next day the two smaller ships were moved out into the bay where they anchored and the big frigate came alongside to start the loading. Although it was not yet completed, Merriman was pleased. He would be free of the shore and his ships victualled with everything needed for months to come.

That evening, Merriman and his selected officers assembled on the quayside where coaches were waiting for them. Much washing and brushing of uniforms and polishing of boots and swords had taken place and Merriman noted that he could certainly be proud of the officers' appearance. The blue and white and gold of the sailors contrasted with the red of the marine captain's coat. The coach horses pulled them up a hill to where a huge mansion, ablaze with lights awaited them. They were greeted by a rotund and magnificently uniformed Major Domo who enquired their names but, like the soldier yesterday, had difficulty with the English and announced them, with much prompting from Humphries, as Captain Merriman and his officers.

Governor Escoveda came forward and introduced the lady on his arm as his wife, the Lady Adelie. He then introduced Merriman to more men dressed in flamboyant uniforms also with their ladies. The welcome that Merriman and his officers received was quite breath-taking - surrounded as they were by the other guests with only a few of them speaking English. Poor Humphries did his best to translate but finally gave up. That did not seem to matter as the chattering continued while Merriman was handed a glass of wine and he looked about him.

Most of the officers seemed to be coping with the confusion of language and the magnificence of the surroundings but the three midshipmen - only boys really - were standing there with mouths agape, each clutching a glass of wine. Merriman was glad he had given them a stern warning about drinking too much and had told the officers to watch them. He suddenly realised that most of the men had left him in a circle of ladies who were vying with each other to catch his eye by smiling at him coquettishly from behind their fans and displaying their barely covered breasts and exotic jewellery.

He smiled and grinned and looked for his officers to see them equally surrounded. Of the midshipmen there was no longer any sign. More drink was offered and Merriman wondered how Stewart was managing to be supplied with water or fruit juice instead of wine. But he had no time to see more as the Major Domo announced in a loud voice that the meal was ready. Merriman had hardly time to move before his arm was grasped by the Lady Adelie to allow him to escort her into the dining room. This was magnificently appointed and lit by what seemed to be hundreds of candles. Fortunately all the doors and windows were wide open to allow the heat to escape.

Merriman found himself seated at the top of the table between the governor and his wife with Humphries next to the lady and Captain Macleod near the governor separated from him by his own wife, Alicia. Merriman's officers were also seated towards the top of the table with the red-faced midshipmen who had now reappeared seated lower down, each of them with a lady seated to either side.

As the meal progressed, dish after dish along with yet more jugs of wine were served by liveried footmen. There was a profusion of different meats. Apart from the expected pork and beef there was chicken, duck and other fowl that Merriman could not identify. Other dishes contained stews and curries and there was fish too and shrimps cooked with vegetables and coconut. After all that, great platters containing at least four or five varieties of fruit and then cheese were brought to the table.

Merriman realised that he was becoming tipsy. Knowing it was likely that he would have to make a speech later, he determined to drink nothing more. He was a representative of his country and it would not do for him to be drunk. That was difficult as wine was continually pressed on him but he refused it all only keeping one glass from which he took only occasional sips.

At last the meal was over and the governor rose to speak. As he did so, the governor's wife changed places with Humphries who moved nearer to Merriman to translate. The governor started talking about how England was Portugal's earliest ally and all officers of His Britannic Majesty's navy were more than welcome. They had saved Portuguese lives and property, killed pirates and recovered ships. He went on to say Humphries was a representative of the British Government and that they had come to destroy more pirates. He droned on and on with Humphries translating only the main points. Eventually he raised his glass and proposed a toast to Merriman and the Royal Navy. Everybody rose to echo the toast and the officers who couldn't understand a word could do no more than copy Merriman who nodded and smiled.

But the governor hadn't finished; he announced that it was his great pleasure to present each of the three captains with an engraved sword with a silver and gold hilt. After that ceremony more toasts were proposed with Merriman drinking only sips of wine. Suddenly Humphries nudged him saying quietly that it was now Merriman's turn. He rose to his feet - rather unsteadily he thought - and smiled round at the company while he tried to remember what he should say.

"Your Excellency Governor Escoveda, ladies and gentlemen. First I must thank you on behalf of my officers and myself for the wonderful gifts of these splendid swords which we shall wear with pride." He paused while Humphries translated his words into Portuguese, the pause giving him time to think. "As your Excellency has said, Portugal and England have been good allies, for some centuries if my memory serves me right, but it was good fortune that my ships arrived when they did."

Portugal was a strongly Catholic country so he added, "Maybe God's hand guided us." There were shouts and murmurs of approval when his words were translated. He continued, "Now I wish to thank you all for the friendliness and welcome we have received. You have a beautiful city and I only wish we could stay longer. So, if my officers will stand and join me in a toast, I propose 'A health to all here and long may your city continue to prosper'." Again Humphries translated, the officers stood and raised their glasses and the room erupted with applause as the guests stood and began to chatter delightedly.

Merriman caught Andrews' eye and with a sideways tilt of his head indicated that they should leave. He had briefed them beforehand so they were expecting it and they moved down to where the midshipmen were sitting with flushed faces, barely managing to keep their eyes open. Merriman had noted that they had all eaten heartily of the many strange dishes of food but he also noted that they were not drunk even though they wobbled a bit as they stood.

He looked for the governor, saw him, and with Humphries he approached to take his leave. The governor was surprised that they were leaving so early but Merriman explained - through Humphries - that they must be aboard their ships ready for tomorrow. He became aware of Captain Macleod nearby and asked him if he would come to the *Lord Stevenage* in the morning with the accounts for payment. The coaches were waiting with the escort of officer and dragoons and they were taken back to the quayside.

Chapter Twelve

Slaves

The next morning, whilst the last loading of the frigate *Lord Stevenage* was being completed, Merriman with Lieutenant De Mowbray and Captain St James of the marines were strolling along the quayside to stretch their legs and to watch some of the activity further along the quay. One of the first things to catch their attention was a dirty, poorly maintained trading vessel tied up alongside with the crew opening the hatches. Immediately a terrible stench assailed their nostrils and all three men took an involuntary step back.

"My God, sir, what foulness is this?" said De Mowbray clutching a kerchief to his nose.

His question was answered immediately by the sight of lines of men in shackles shuffling onto the quayside, urged on by the whips of the crew. All of them were negroes and judging from the barely healed scars on their backs, most of them had been whipped many times. A man in a threadbare coat with the remains of some gold braid and lace still clinging to it, approached the three officers and said, "Interested are you, gentlemen? You'll have to wait until my cargo is cleaned up and in the slave market before you can buy any of them."

"No, we are not, but I would like to see the market you speak of. Where is it?" Merriman asked.

"Further along to the lower part of the town over there, but the sale on right now must be nearly over so you'll have to hurry if you want to buy slaves."

Merriman, like the others was holding his kerchief to his nose, said, "I hate the idea, gentlemen, but I must see what is going on, I think it will make my mind up about an idea I have."

They walked in the direction the slaver captain had indicated and became aware of screams and shouts and more of the stench coming from a building with all windows and doors secured by iron bars. Behind the bars could be seen the desperate and anguished faces of black men and women. Some black men - also obviously slaves - were carrying buckets of ordure out of the building and tipping it into a pit. Others were carrying buckets of water to swill out the floors of the cells. Even as they watched, one of the barred gates opened and two white men appeared dragging a group of four negroes, three men and a woman, all stark naked apart from their chains, up to a low platform which they were forced on to. A man standing behind a sort of lectern began to shout to the assembled crowd.

"Fine new merchandise, gentlemen, from Africa they are and all fit for work where you want them." He nodded to one of the guards who prodded the slaves with a stick to make them turn round and then made them flex their arms to show how well-muscled they were. "Strong men you see, gentlemen, and the woman is a peach." He nodded to the guard who began to fondle her breasts, lifting them up to show their fullness and then he dragged her upright by her hair to show her full body to the potential buyers.

"I've seen enough," said a horrified Merriman. "Back to the ship now, gentlemen."

"I've never seen anything like it, sir, it was a terrible sight. No wonder men in our government want it to be stopped," said an ashen-faced De Mowbray. "It made me feel quite sick."

"It shows you what some men will stoop to, John. Of course we have all seen slaves in the Caribbean islands but I have never seen the indignities forced upon them like this, but I suppose it must happen there," Merriman said sadly.

"It does, sir," said St James, shaking his head. "I've seen it myself."

On board the ship, Merriman asked the two officers down to his cabin and ordered the officer of the watch to call Captains Andrews and Stewart over for a conference. "And ask Mr Humphries and the First Lieutenant to join us as well."

In the great cabin Merriman shouted, "Peters, bring brandy

at once. You'll both join me in a glass I trust, gentlemen? It will help us to dispel the sights we have just seen."

Humphries joined them and gladly took a glass himself. In only a few minutes more, Andrews and Stewart also joined them eager to know what Merriman wanted them for.

Merriman drew a deep breath and began to relate to them all that had been seen that morning. "It confirms to me what I had almost decided upon yesterday. We have a lot of prisoners below decks, by my count some twenty four Spanish, thirty native Indians and thirteen others captured from the privateers. I had you keep them below for a good reason. As I told some of you earlier, we cannot hand the Spanish men over to the Portuguese to hang or to make slaves of, if that reached the ears of the Spanish in Buenos Aires where some of their fleet may lie, it could mean war. After all there is a fragile peace between them at the moment which allows trading. The native Indians were forced to work as crew on that old frigate, slaves really, so I cannot and will not send them ashore to be subjected to the horrors we have seen in the slave market. The privateers are different and yet I do not want to submit them to the horror of slavery. I propose that we shall deal with them differently."

"I wondered what you were keeping them for, sir," said Andrews. "So what will we do with them?

"This is what I propose we do, gentlemen. On our way south we will send the Spanish ashore, well away from any Portuguese settlements or villages. We will give them a boat with some oars and a scrap of sail and water and a few provisions. Some weapons can be left for them to use for hunting and to protect themselves against animals and Indians. We shall do the same with the Indians, but before that I will ask Captain Macleod if he can speak their tongue. If one or two of them can help us to get to Montevideo and find Don Galliano and capture him, so much the better."

"Well, that will solve that problem, sir, but what about the real privateers or pirates?"

"I will send them ashore and ask – as is my duty - that they be hanged," replied Merriman. "They deserve no pity after what they have done."

He was interrupted by the marine sentry knocking and announcing that Captain Macleod wished to see him. "Exactly on cue, gentlemen. Send him in, sentry," he called.

When the man entered, Peters offered him a brandy which he gladly accepted. Then, looking round at the officers assembled round the table, he asked, "You all look very serious, gentlemen, may I know what has happened to make you so?"

Merriman told him what had been decided to do with the prisoners and asked, "Do you see any difficulties with that, sir?"

The Captain shook his head ruefully. "Only that Governor Escoveda knows that there are prisoners and is looking forward to seeing them hanged although he knows that it might cause war with Spain. He feels that with the Royal Navy here to protect Portuguese possessions, war might be welcome."

"Well, he must be told that we shall not be here for long and we do not want to be the cause of war between you and Spain. Perhaps I should go and see him?"

"It might be best, sir. I have told him that your ships will not be here for long but coming from you he may be more inclined to believe it. If you tell him that you are leaving him some pirates to hang it, will temper his disappointment."

"Very well, Captain. As you may know we took many rolls of expensive cloth from the frigate and boxes of silver. The cloth you may keep and if I give the governor some of the silver, that too may temper his disappointment. The rest I will keep as my ship's prize to be sold. I shall go promptly to see the governor if I could use your carriage? Now, before I go, I must pay you what we owe. if only for the stuff you bought from outlying farms."

"Thank you, sir," said Macleod. "As you know we have a good number of the prisoners aboard that captured pirate ship, are you taking them with you?"

"Yes, I propose to take that ship with us with your own crew aboard to sail her. Now that we have taken so much water and supplies on board, we have kept the Spanish in poor conditions because of lack of space, so some of them can be transferred to that ship. I'll send some marines with them to guard them. After that, Captain, your own men can sail it back here and you can keep it."

"Thank you, Captain, thank you. In that case I will go with my men to sail back."

"Good. Now I asked you before if you could speak any of the native language and you said maybe a bit. So I would be pleased if you would try and talk to any of them that might be prepared to help us in the capture of the privateers' leader, Don Galliano who imprisoned them. You can tell them that they will all be released afterwards. You see, my intent is to go and capture the rogue and burn or sink as many of his ships as possible. Also I have only some not very accurate charts of this coast, especially in the Rio de la Plata and near Montevideo. Can you help me with that?"

"Indeed I can, sir. We trade with the Spanish down there and I have good charts. I will have them copied for you."

By the first light of dawn of the following day, the four ships were leaving Salvador and quickly heading south with a good wind behind them. All had been completed as arranged and Merriman's sailing master was delighted with the new charts which had been copied again and again so that each ship had its own.

Merriman called for Captain Almeida to have his chains removed and be brought aft. When he arrived in a dirty and dishevelled condition, Merriman had him sit while Peters brought him a drink. Almeida eyed it warily before speaking. "Thank you, sir, and may I ask what you intend to do with us?"

"You are to be released a few hundred miles south of here with a boat, water and supplies. We will provide some basic tools and weapons as well. It is up to you to decide where to go, but I suggest you go south to find more of your countrymen."

Captain Almeida looked amazed. "We had not expected that, sir. We thought we would be sent ashore to be hanged or sold into slavery. Why are you doing this?"

"If you were to be hanged or sold and Spain found out, it could provoke a war between you and the Portuguese which would be of no benefit to anybody. So you and your men will go ashore, perhaps three or four hundred miles south of here, and the Indians - your slaves - will be released even further south. Now I have a question for you. What do you know of the treaty proposed by Napoleon Buonaparte? When I left England it seemed likely that the preliminary details were being discussed but many people in our government are against it, but I know no more."

"A treaty, Captain? I can hardly believe it. I have heard nothing but I will say that if that is what that man is proposing then it will be of benefit to nobody but himself. Perhaps he wants a respite from war to raise more soldiers and their equipment?"

"Yes, maybe, that is what many men of our government think but there are more who favour a treaty but until we hear more we must remain enemies Captain Almeida."

As arranged, the Spanish prisoners were released on a deserted part of the coast. Macleod had suggested several places which would be suitable. "Some places won't do, Captain," he said. "As I expect you know, we do have the odd problem with some of the native tribes who come from inland to attack the smallest of our settlements and villages before disappearing back into the rainforest. A small party of men will have to be careful and use their boat as much as possible. In many places the forest reaches almost down to the shore but elsewhere the coast is backed by scrubland and desert."

Merriman took Macleod's advice and put the Spanish men ashore in one of their own boats from the sunken frigate, equipped just as Merriman had ordered. The last to go into the boat was Captain Almeida. Merriman had ordered a full side party of marines and bos'n's mates with whistles as the Captain saw with amazement. He turned to Merriman and said, with tears in his eyes, "Thank you, Captain, for the honour you have given me. You are a true English gentleman; would you shake hands with your prisoner before I go? And may I say that I have never seen such a fine ship as you have. If the rest of the Royal Navy is like this, the Spanish Navy will without doubt be in trouble."

They shook hands, Almeida climbed down and, once they

had landed safely, Merriman ordered sail to be set. Then he watched silently as the land disappeared on the starboard quarter. With the Spanish out of the *Lord Stevenage,* Merriman had been able to have the Indians brought on board and the captured privateer sent back to Salvador with a happy Captain Macleod waving farewell. He had convinced two of the Indians to help Merriman and, when their comrades had been landed as promised, Merriman kept them to help. It transpired that one of them spoke some Spanish and Humphries was soon in conversation with him.

Chapter Thirteen

Plans for Action at Montevideo

The flotilla proceeded south, well out of sight of land to avoid any Spanish warships there may be, although Captain Almeida had said that most of them were unseaworthy and stayed within the Rio de la Plata. Some were at Buenos Aires and most at Montevideo, with only the occasional ship from Spain or France appearing. It seemed as though Spain had too many problems with the French at home to spare much thought for her colonies and the shipyard was fast running out of supplies including canvas and cordage and other essential supplies.

After much more thought Merriman signalled to both ships for their captains to join him. Merriman met them in his cabin with Mr Humphries and, after all were supplied with a drink, he said, with a twinkle in his eye, "I have determined on a plan for what to do when we are near to our destination, gentlemen."

Andrews replied immediately, "I know that look of old, sir. I know you will have a good plan."

"Yes, here is the outline of what I propose. First, do you know of any men in your crew who can speak French? I can find three but for the plan to succeed I need more."

Both thought for a few moments before nodding. "I have two or three, sir, together with two of my officers that will be five," said Andrews.

"And I think I have two, sir, and my second lieutenant as well," said Stewart.

"Very good, that gives us five men plus three from this ship, and three officers, total eleven. It should be enough. I propose that your ship, David, be altered back to look like a French ship. After all she is French built and the fastest of the three of us. The name will be repainted to the original and, although I know you won't like it, the decks and running rigging must look dirty and slovenly. You will have the sailmakers from all three ships to alter the sails we took off the frigate to make them fit your yards. That canvas is old, dirty and patched so will I hope give the impression of a ship manned by French revolutionaries who think themselves equal to the officers and are slow to obey orders. Mr Humphries, with your excellent French I would like you to play the part of the captain with you, David, out of sight but able to tell Mr Humphries what to order the men to do. Nobody should wear any blue coats and the marines must be in their shirtsleeves. Is that all clear, gentlemen?"

He was rewarded by nods all round.

"Good. Now then, I am sending your ship because it is the most suitable and you will appreciate that I must stay behind with other two. *Eagle* should fly the French flag, the Tricolour, when in sight of land. Have you one still aboard, David?"

"Yes, sir, there is a selection of foreign flags in the locker."

"Good, now whilst *Lord Stevenage* and *The Mayfly* stay well off shore out of the estuary of the river, *Eagle* will proceed up river to look at Montevideo which we know is the main Spanish harbour in the River Plate. If you can determine how many warships and possible privateers are there, you will then return and join us out at sea. If it is at all possible you must land Mr Humphries near the town for him to carry out his own investigations. Mr Humphries, I propose that we call all the French speakers to this ship and you can help them with the language. You see if anyone hails *Eagle* the reply must be in French. It could be more than two weeks before we are down there so you will have time to do all that."

Chapter Fourteen

Improving Swordsmanship

The next weeks passed slowly. Nothing was sighted and the weather remained fair. Mr Humphries was busy improving the language of the French speakers who had been gathered together in a regular class on the gun deck. The midshipmen were undergoing their daily lessons in arithmetic and use of navigation instruments but for Merriman and his officers there was little to do except the usual exercises, deck watches and the continual look for anything wrong with the ship. Boredom began to creep in until Merriman, looking round his cabin, saw the three swords hanging on the cabin bulkhead.

One was the lavishly decorated and engraved sword presented to him by the Honourable East India Company for his exploits in the Indian Ocean nearly two years ago and which he would have had done better to leave at home. One was his usual dress sword while the third and heavier one was the one he used for real fighting. The swords caused him to remember the fencing lessons he used to have with the Marine Captain St James who was an accomplished swordsman. He determined that all officers should have more practice in the use of their weapon.

"Mr St James, Edward, I have had no lessons with you for weeks on the use of the sword so I think that your teaching should continue, but with a difference. Apart from my practice I want you to take every officer on deck in turn to see how proficient they are with the sword and see what you can do to improve them. I propose that you and I start now with the others watching",

"Aye-aye, sir," replied the marine. "I look forward to that. I think we both may be a little rusty on the finer points. I will pass the word to the officers to fetch my sword and meet you on deck."

A few minutes later, Merriman and St James faced each other on the quarter deck with an interested group of officers watching. After the usual moves with the swords in salute they started. There was no noise except the clash of steel on steel and heavy breathing of the two men. They continued until St James pierced Merriman's sleeve without touching his arm and they stood back.

"Well you had me there, Edward. If I had been an enemy I would now be dead," said Merriman.

"Yes, sir, you were a little slow with that last riposte but otherwise I think you have remembered most of what I taught you. With your permission, sir, I'll try somebody else now."

At Merriman's nod he called the first lieutenant to try his luck. They fought for three or four minutes until St James called a halt. "Mr Merryweather is very good, sir, there isn't much more I can teach him but there are some points needing practice."

"Very good, Edward, have a drink and a rest for your arm before you try somebody else. I suggest our two newest officers, Mr Bristow and Mr De Mowbray."

"Yes, sir. Mr Bristow, will you try?"

Bristow came forward but it soon became clear that he was totally overmatched and had a lot to learn. The next was De Mowbray and from the moment the blades crossed it was evident that he was an accomplished swordsman. The moves were so rapid, too fast for the eye to follow, until once again St James drew back.

"By God, Mr De Mowbray, you nearly had me there. Captain, sir, I thought I had nothing to learn but Mr De Mowbray is as good if not better than I am. Remember, gentlemen, the old saying, no skill in swordsmanship however just, can guard against a madman's thrust, which means that you must beware of the man who doesn't care if he dies as long as he can kill you."

"Very well then, gentlemen," said Merriman, "it seems that we now have two fencing masters so that we can increase the number of lessons, after all it may save your life one day. Now the rest of you let us see what you can do."

The other officers came forward one by one with varying degrees of success. Shrigley was quite competent as was Lieutenant Goodwin of the marines but all needed some more expert tuition.

Merriman said, "That settles the matter, gentlemen, all of you must practice every day as often as duties allow with one of our two experts and that includes me as a pupil. Mr De Mowbray, I look to you to make a roster of lessons bearing in mind that men will be on their usual duties, and you could include the midshipmen, their use of their dirks may save their life one day."

"Aye-aye, sir, and if I may be so bold as to suggest that many of the petty officers and crew could also do with more instruction. I know a cutlass is not suitable for the fencing we have been doing but some more defensive moves could be learned."

"Excellent, Mr De Mowbray, perhaps you gentlemen will sort it out together."

Many of the crew had been watching from various vantage points and an excited chattering broke out at Merriman's words. And so, as the ship moved ever southwards, the lessons began. The men eagerly joined in, all recognising the need for it.

After some days Merriman sent De Mowbray over to *Eagle* with orders to Captain Andrews to do the same to improve the skill of his men.

Eventually the flotilla arrived near to the River Plate but well out of sight of land and Merriman called the captains to him. Final details were settled; the French speaking officers and men had been transferred to *Eagle* some days ago and were all aware of what they had to do. The spare men from *Eagle* had been taken on board the other two ships. Merriman was keenly aware that he was sending the ship and men into what could well be a very dangerous situation - the lion's mouth as it were - but could think of nothing more to do to improve the chances of success. *Eagle* had been completely transformed and anyone could see that she was clearly a French ship. After a brief hand clasp with Merriman and Stewart, Captain Andrews and Mr Humphries were taken back to the ship and *Eagle* moved westward to the estuary of the River Plate.

Chapter Fifteen

Punishment

Amongst all the excitement, Merriman had not forgotten the supposed murder of two of his men and as soon as the corvette disappeared he called for Merryweather to see if he had heard anything more about the suspected murder.

"I questioned petty officers, especially the mate who saw what happened. Three men had been sent up the foremast to check on the fore tops'ls yard to check & tighten sail gaskets if found to be necessary and only one had come down again, sir. I have spoken to all the ships' officers, and they in turn to the bos'n's mates and others but nobody could say that they had seen what happened, sir. But there are some rumours that one of the new men has been throwing his weight around and beating any man who disagrees with him. The two missing men, both new at Portsmouth at the same time as the bully, tried to stand up to him - as did many others - but he was always at odds with most of them and making wild threats. He is a good seaman, sir, but always slow and reluctant to obey orders."

"I see, Henry, what is the man's name?"

"Egling, sir. I think he is a Kentish man as were the other two. Come to think about it all three were unusually eager to sign on for the King's shilling. Perhaps they were trying to escape from the law for theft or murder ashore, sir, and were arguing about loot or who had killed somebody."

"Well he seems to be the most likely suspect. After all, most of the men have been with me for years and apart from minor fights and disagreements, we have had no trouble," said Merriman walking round the cabin and tugging his ear, the usual sign of deep thought. "Very well, Henry, will you pass the word for Mr Shrigley and Captain St James to come and join us."

When they arrived Merriman and Merryweather told them all about what was suspected of the man Egling and that he was going to have a jury of the three of them to speak with him and call some of the mates to give evidence of his behaviour.

"Mr Merryweather, you know which of the mates could be relied on to state facts about the man. Have them gathered in the officers' wardroom until we call for them, and be quiet about it so as not to alarm the fellow. Mr St James, you will not be part of the jury but select your sergeant and two other steady marines and have them ready to bring Egling here when I call."

"Aye-aye, sir," they both replied and disappeared to do what Merriman had ordered.

Then he called for his clerk Tomkins and told him what was going to happen. "I want you to sit in that corner and take as many notes as you can about what everyone says. Afterwards you can ask us any questions to be sure you have the report down correctly."

Tomkins nodded and went to fetch writing materials.

Merriman said, "A bad business, Mr Shrigley, murder if it is murder and by now the man probably thinks he has got away with it. If he is guilty we shall have to have another hanging and I do so hate hangings."

"Yes, sir, I don't like them either but regulations prescribe it. Just like it did for the man who tried to kill you when we were at Copenhagen."

They didn't have long to wait before the two officers returned to report that everything was ready.

"Right, gentlemen, bring your chairs round to this side of the table to face the man, and Mr St James, have your men find him and bring him here."

Eventually there was the sound of scuffling and shouting outside and the door was thrown open by the sentry to reveal three marines, the sergeant and two men struggling to control the man Egling. Not until the sentry pricked him in the throat with his fixed bayonet did he quieten down and was dragged in to face the three serious-faced officers in front of him.

"Now then, Egling," said Merriman, "we are not accusing

you of anything – yet, but we believe you were involved in the disappearance of two of your crewmates when you were all on the fore mainyard during the storm weeks ago. What do you have to say?"

"It's a lie, sir, who could see anything on that night with all t'spray and such. I were up there but I'd finished my side of the yard an' I left the other two up there and came down. Dunno' what they did but they didn't follow me down."

"I see, Egling, but what if I told you that you were seen to attack them with a knife by one of the mates up the mainmast, what do you say to that?"

"It's all lies, that's what, like I said you couldn't see anything up there and anyway all of the mates 'ave 'ad it in for me since I came aboard."

"I'll have some of the mates in shortly," said Merriman. "Tell me, what happened to your knife, did you stab somebody with it?"

"Dunno, sir, I lost it long ago during the storm, I think," replied the man.

"Then why did you not apply to the Purser for another one? Was it perhaps that you didn't want to draw attention to its loss?"

Egling hung his head. "Dunno, sir," was all he said.

"Mr Merryweather, would you bring the witnesses up from the wardroom and line them up outside in the order you believe we should see them, please."

Merryweather was soon back and nodded to Merriman.

"Please bring in the first witness, Mr Merryweather, if you please."

The first to appear was master's mate Harriman who stood there nervously twisting his woollen cap in his hands.

"Mr Harriman, please tell us what you believed you saw the night two men disappeared," asked Merriman.

Harriman gulped, took a deep breath, glanced at Egling and started. "Well, sir, it were like this. Mr 'Enderson sent me aloft to check on the mainyard chains - 'e thought they were loose - and when I were there I saw three men on the foreyard, in a group, sir, and they seemed to be fighting. I couldn't see clearly who they were, sir, but I think one of them were that man Egling."

"Thank you, Mr Harriman. Anything else?"

"Well, sir, many days later I heard that Egling came down alone and the others must 'ave gone overboard. But I couldn't see 'im clearly enough to swear it were Egling so I said nothing until Mr Merryweather asked me about it."

"Thank you, Mr Harriman. You may go. Mr Merryweather, will you call your next witnesses?"

"Yes, sir. May I say that they are all reliable men, petty officers, who will tell us what they have seen and heard on the lower decks."

The men were called one after the other and confirmed their knowledge of Egling's behaviour, fighting and beating any who disagreed with him and that the two missing men were always arguing with him. The three of them all came aboard just before the ship sailed and there was bad blood between them and men had wondered why they almost ran aboard.

"P'raps they were escaping from somewhere," said the last witness.

During this recital of events, Egling's face became greyer and greyer, but he made a tentative attempt to defend himself by saying, "There ain't no real evidence against me, it's all lies it is. I agree we came 'ere in an 'urry, we 'ad stolen some money and a man was killed by one of the other two and the justices were after us, but that don't prove I killed anyone."

"Thank you, sergeant, take the prisoner out but keep him isolated nearby until I call for him."

"Aye-aye, sir. Right you men, you 'eard the captain, take 'im out."

When they had taken the swearing and shouting Egling out, Merriman said, "Gentlemen, we now have to discuss the evidence given and decide on a verdict. What do you think, Henry?"

Merryweather began to speak. "Well, sir, much of the evidence is inconclusive. We have heard that he is a bad character but that is only hearsay for the most part and means nothing. However I am tempted to believe Harriman's evidence and other things such as the loss of Egling's knife which he can't explain. But the main point against him is own admission that the three of them attempted robbery and a man was killed. Doesn't that mean that even if he didn't kill the man he is guilty with them anyway, sir?"

"What do you think about this, Alfred?" asked Merriman of Shrigley.

"I must say that I agree with Mr Merryweather, but I don't know if he is considered guilty of murder just by being with the men who did it. Maybe Mr De Mowbray can help us here, I know his father is a lawyer and some of the law may have rubbed off on him."

"Excellent idea, Alfred." Merriman raised his voice and called out for the lieutenant to be summoned. When De Mowbray appeared, Merriman said, "As you may be aware we are sitting here as a jury and we are unsure about a point of law and hope that with your father being a lawyer you might be able to help us. The problem is this." He outlined the evidence they had heard.

"Well, sir," the lieutenant replied after listening closely, "I remember going to court with my father to listen to several cases. He wanted me to be a lawyer like him but I wanted to go to sea, which is why I am here, sir. However I do remember one or two cases of men being accused of murder telling the court that it was other men in a gang who did the murder." He took a little while to think and then said, "I am certain there is a law called Guilt by Association and all the men were convicted and hanged because of it."

"Do we take it that if a group of men attempt a robbery, even the man who may be holding their horses outside is considered guilty of the crime also?"

"Yes, sir, I remember that clearly," replied the lieutenant.

"Thank you, Mr De Mowbray," said Merriman. "You may go." When they were alone again, Merriman turned to the others and said, "I think that is now clear, gentlemen. By his own admission he was with the other two when they committed murder and he is guilty of that. Therefore it seems a safe assumption that he did kill the others to prevent them accusing him of the murder. What say you? Each of you must judge for yourselves and give me a verdict before I give you mine. Lieutenant Merryweather?"

"If what we learn from De Mowbray is correct then my verdict is guilty, sir."

"Lieutenant Shrigley, what say you?"

"Guilty, sir, and even if we can't prove he killed the other two men on the yard he is definitely guilty of murder ashore, sir."

"That is my conclusion also, gentlemen. Now we must do what we have to do and convict the fellow. Alfred, be good enough to call in the prisoner and the marines."

When Egling was dragged in by the marines under the close orders of St James, Merriman, with a face like stone, said, "Egling, we have considered all that we have learned from the witnesses and yourself. From your own mouth you said that you were with the other two men when they committed murder which in law makes you equally guilty. That law is named Guilt by Association. Have you anything to say before I pass sentence?"

The wretched man shook his head and stared at the deck beneath his feet.

"Very well then, Egling, you are charged with murder both ashore and on this ship and there is only one punishment for that as laid down in King's Regulations. Death. You have a half hour to make your peace with whatever God you have and then you will be hanged. Take him away."

And so, half an hour later, Egling was dragged up on deck to where all hands had been called to witness punishment. The officers and the rest of the marines looked on from the quarterdeck as the bos'n adjusted the noose around the man's neck.

Merriman raised his voice. "This man has been found guilty of murder both ashore and on this ship for which there is only one punishment decreed in the King's Regulations and that is

Death."

He proceeded to read aloud the appropriate chapter of Regulations and then said, "Carry on, Mr Brockle."

The bos'n turned to the men holding the tail of the rope and shouted, "Ready, heave away." To the rattle of the marine drummer's drum, Egling was hauled aloft where he struggled and kicked for several minutes before finally hanging there lifeless. He was lowered down to where the doctor pronounced that life was extinct. The sailmaker produced a piece of canvas to sew the body in and Merriman said sombrely to Merryweather, "Dismiss all hands and then join me in my cabin and bring Mr Shrigley with you."

Below he called for his servant to bring the brandy out and then collapsed into his chair motioning to the others to do the same. "A hateful business, gentlemen, but we really had no choice. I hope this excellent brandy will cheer us up a little."

Chapter Sixteen

Montevideo

The corvette *Eagle* slowly made its way up the River Plate towards Montevideo harbour and, as the days passed, Captain Andrews and Mr Humphries repeatedly told the men what was expected to happen and the French speakers rehearsed again and again.

It was Andrew's intention to arrive in Montevideo harbour bay at dusk, flying the Tricolour to deceive any onlookers that the ship really was French. The ship, by now reduced to a single jib and tops'ls, crept slowly into the bay. Behind the promontory to the south east the town with its harbour revealed itself. With his glass Andrews could see a selection of small sloops and brigs moored closely together. As he took note of how many, he saw the ship which had followed the flotilla for so long. Most of the ships had some of their sails hanging to dry as did the one he recognised of which he could see the distinctive tops'ls quite clearly.

On the other side of the bay he could see three Spanish warships, a frigate and two seventy fours, all in bad shape with no yards crossed and rigging hanging slack. Indeed there was another one which had evidently sunk at her mooring; all that could be seen were the tops of the lower masts. Just before the light disappeared completely, Andrews had the ship anchored and all sails reefed in a slovenly manner.

Just as the ship came to rest, a small boat appeared and an enquiry was shouted in Spanish and a kind of fractured French as to how long they would be there. Humphries replied that they would only be there for one or two days while some repairs were carried out and they would be going further up river to Buenos Aires, the capital. That seemed to satisfy the officer in what was evidently a guard boat and it moved away into the darkness towards the town.

Andrews retired to his cabin and mulled over what he had seen then called his officers and Humphries together to tell them what he had decided. His first lieutenant, Peter Davies, was accompanied by lieutenants Scott and Duddy, together with the French-speaking officers from the flotilla, all eager to know what their Captain had decided to do.

He began, "You know that Montevideo is the principal Spanish port and harbour in this river and you have seen the condition of their ships which are surely in as bad a condition as the frigate we sank. I don't believe they represent any threat to us or our other ships. Mr Humphries, I know you are wanting to go ashore to find out what you can about the conditions here and anything you can learn about any Spanish activity which may affect England and our navy. So I suggest we put you ashore in another hour or so in a dark place. Your boat crew should all be French speakers of course and they can wait for you. When we know what Mr Humphries has discovered we can plan further ahead."

Humphries returned before dawn, quietly satisfied with what he had discovered. In Andrew's cabin, holding a well-deserved mug of hot coffee, he related all that he had found. "I went to the dockyard first and things are in a terrible state there. The men off the ships and the workers ashore are all completely fed up with their conditions. They have no rope of any kind and no spare canvas either. The ships need re-fitting before going out to sea again and they cannot do it. Two of them need hauling out to be careened and timber replaced as well. I spoke to many of the men in French and poor Spanish and most of them spent most of their time in the many taverns there, when they have money that is, which is in short supply. They haven't been paid for months. Spain seems to have forgotten them. Their morale is at rock bottom. Oh and another point, the forts ashore are not manned because they do not have enough men or powder."

"Did you get near enough to the ships we believe to be privateers to make any judgement about their condition?" asked

Andrews.

"Yes, though I could not see not too much other than that they are moored close together, in fact several of them are tied alongside each other. There are nine or ten of them. I spoke to some men in a tavern and they said that one of their ships had come back to report an English fleet cruising down the coast but they didn't seem concerned."

"I think that will help us. I have the beginnings of a plan but I need to know where we could find that man Don Galiano. You do not know his whereabouts, do you?"

"No. I made a few cautious enquiries but all I learned is that he has a house in the town though another thing I was told is that the town will be holding a fiesta tomorrow which will continue into the night. That may give us the opportunity to find him."

"Thank you, now I suggest you get some sleep. We will talk again."

When it was light enough to see, Andrews sent men aloft to replace some ropes and send down a sail for repair. Others began chipping at paintwork ready for repainting and two men were over the side on the harbour side scraping and painting parts of the hull. Of course the ropes and the sail were all in good order but Andrews was determined to give the impression of repairing as the guard boat had been told. The men worked listlessly so that anybody watching from the harbour would see that their hearts were not on their work.

Early that morning, several small boats put out from the harbour and approached the corvette to sell produce, fruit and bread, piglets and chickens, and bottles of locally brewed rum. Thanks to Merriman's foresight there were enough men on deck able to speak French and, with the help of Humphries and his mixed up Spanish, they were able to buy plenty of fresh food, gold bought anything it seemed. Another larger boat came alongside but this one was markedly different. There were several women aboard and it was obvious what kind they were. Humphries soon told them to clear off and sent them packing with the threat of dropping a cannon ball into the boat.

Mid-morning Mr Humphries, with the two Indians came on

deck and the Indians soon began to chatter excitedly. They pointed to the shore and told Humphries where the Galiano house was situated. He questioned them more and then turned to Andrews who was making a show of coiling carelessly stowed ropes.

"Captain, they know which is Galiano's house. It's that one painted green inside the walls of the town, easy to see because all the other houses near to it are painted white or yellow or ochre. They are certain of that because they were house slaves there before they were flogged and sold to the Spanish to work aboard the frigate we sank."

"Good, can they draw some kind of a plan of the property do you think?" asked Andrews.

"I'll see to that. It could be helpful if we are to go there to find him."

In the event the ex-slaves were able to give Humphries all the information he needed to draw a map himself of the outside and of the lower floor of the house. "There is a wall round it only about six feet high with a wide gate at the front and a small gate in the wall at the back for food and such to be taken to the kitchen," he said. "The slaves are locked into a shed at night but the key hangs on a nail near to the door. There are two guards with dogs patrolling inside the wall at night. There are four guards who take their duty in pairs alternately and their quarters are by the front gate. Another thing, when the town had the last fiesta, Galiano didn't go as he hates the noise and spent time at home in his house with friends, drinking heavily, so we may hope that he will be at home tonight."

Chapter Seventeen

A Prisoner Taken

Andrews called all the officers down to his cabin to discuss his ideas. "From what we have already learned, gentlemen, it might not be too difficult to capture Galiano. If we wait until the fiesta is at its loudest, which will be in the evening and into the night, we should be able to take a boat to the harbour and small party of us can go through the town gate with the aim of reaching the house without any alarm being raised."

"Who will go, sir?" asked Lieutenant Davis, Andrews' first lieutenant.

"Well not you, Peter. I must leave you in charge of the ship. None of you gentlemen know this Galiano by sight but I do. I saw him in Jamaica. I will take the cutter with a landing party of say, six men, with one other officer. I think Mr Lester from the *Mayfly* and of course our two native Indians with Mr Humphries. That will be a total of eleven to go ashore which should be enough. There will be three other men to stay with the boat and to pretend to be drunk if anybody approaches. We must be as quick as we can and back to the boat."

He paused to see if there were any immediate questions before continuing, "All of the men with me must be French speakers, with enough French speakers left aboard in case any more boats come a calling in the night with any kind of invitation, female or otherwise, which must be chased away. And all of us must be in rough sailors' shirts and trousers with neckerchiefs or cloths to be pulled over our faces to act as disguise. Is all that clear then? Have any of you any questions?"

Heads were nodded in understanding with no questions asked.

"Very well then, once we have returned to the ship, I further propose to up anchor and sail up river in the morning but only far enough to make any watcher think we have left. Then back downstream, with all guns loaded, we will sail past the privateers and blow them to matchwood before moving down to seaward."

That raised eyebrows and an excited chatter.

"Enough, gentlemen. As you leave please ask the gunner to come down to see me."

When Menzies - a grizzled old seaman and a worried man – arrived, obviously thinking he had done something wrong, Andrews reassured him and told him what he wanted. "When I was first lieutenant aboard Captain Merriman's ship in the Baltic we had to burn a plague ship without going near it and this is what we did. We filled bottles with lantern oil and sealed them with rags with a fuse of more oil-soaked rag hanging out. Then they were wrapped in more oiled rags to make them fit snugly into the cannon bore before we put them in the guns ready to fire. As the guns fired, the oil-soaked rag fuse lit and the bottles smashed onto the deck of the plague ship setting it afire. The guns would be loaded as normal with the bottles in last. Do you get the idea, Mr Menzies?"

"Aye, sir, I do," said the man excitedly. "But at what range will we be shooting, sir?"

"As close as possible. Say between twenty five and thirty five yards, I think, so it is up to you to work out the suitable charges for the guns. Use the English powder not the Spanish stuff which is unreliable. I want to set fire to as many of the privateers as we can. I will instruct my servant to let you have all the empty wine bottles from the wardroom and my own store, right?"

"Aye-aye, sir," said Menzies with a grin on his face as he left.

That evening, in the darkness, the boat left the *Eagle* and approached the beach near the harbour, not far from the gateway into the town. The landing party quickly disembarked with one man carrying a bundle of canvas containing their weapons. As they neared the gateway in the ruinous town wall they began laughing and giggling, pretending to drink from rum bottles and flasks with one or two of them being supported by their mates. It would have been apparent to any watcher that they were all drunk. They passed into the town with no difficulty, indeed the two Spanish soldiers on guard duty, also drinking, happily waved them through.

The centre of the town was ablaze with the light from candles and lanterns. Decorative Chinese fireworks shot up into the night sky where they made a grand display of colourful stars as they exploded, the noise being near to deafening. There were few people about in the street, most of them no doubt at the town centre, the focal point for the fireworks and religious processions.

As Andrews and his party moved up the street to the alley which led to the rear of Don Galiano's house, people could be seen up in the town square singing, dancing and drinking with no thought other than to enjoy themselves. The new but as yet unfinished cathedral could easily be seen in the bright light.

Silently the men crept up to the gate in the wall at the back of the house where two of them lifted a third to look over the gate. All was silent apart from some heavy snoring coming from the small hut inside in the shadow of the wall and there was no sign of a dog. The weapons were distributed and one man was helped over the wall to open the gate before they all slipped inside. The drunken gatekeeper was quickly overcome, tied and gagged and the gate bolted again.

Andrews looked at his map, which was easily visible in the light from the fiesta, and pointed to a door at the top of a short flight of steps. Strangely the door was not locked. It opened easily leading into a short passage leading to the kitchen of the house. Two native Indian kitchen slaves were inside, preparing bottles and glasses on one tray and foodstuffs on another. The startled pair both looked up as the Indians and Humphries stepped in making the universal gesture for silence with his finger to his lips. The two men were too surprised to react and were swiftly bound and gagged before they were questioned.

After a quiet discussion, Humphries said, "These two know

our own two Indians and will keep quiet."

The gags were removed and they, Humphries and the four Indians talked in hushed tones together for a few moments.

"What have you learned from these men, Mr Humphries?" asked Andrews.

"Plenty, sir, they are the only two left to serve Galiano, all the others are locked into the slave quarters. Galiano was expecting a lady - well a woman. She arrived earlier and they are upstairs in his bedroom. The food and wine are for later and there is nobody else in the house."

"Excellent, that will make it easier for us to capture him."

Andrews peered out of the kitchen doorway into a lavishly decorated hall with two ornate doors at the far end which must form the front entrance. A stairway led upwards. There was no sound at all from the house to indicate if Galiano was indeed in his bedroom or elsewhere.

"You two men, go over to the front doors there and make sure they are locked and bolted. You two, gag those Indian servants and stay with them and our own two. Now, gentlemen, we will go up and find our target, but silently mind you."

On the landing they were faced by six doorways which must lead into bedrooms. All but one stood open. Andrews crept closer and listened. It was obvious what was going on inside for he could hear squeals and cries from a woman and grunts and gasps from a man as well as squeaks from the bedsprings as they were tested to their limit.

Andrews whispered, "We'll give them another minute then we go in with our neckerchiefs over our faces. We'll seize them and gag them. No talking, but I must see the man's face to be sure we have the right man. Is that all clear?"

All nodded, nervously clutching their swords. Andrews flung open the door and the men rushed in to pounce on the couple in the bed. Then there were different grunts and squeals but the couple stood no chance. Both were easily gagged and tied, still naked.

Andrews looked carefully at the man's face, then nodded. It was Galiano. They left the woman on the bed but untied Galiano and forced him into his trousers and a shirt left lying on a chair as well as some shoes, before tying him up again.

Carrying the struggling man, they went down to the kitchen and put him in a chair. Andrews beckoned to one of the seamen.

"Knock Galiano out then take off his gag," he said. "Then two of you can carry him with us. It will seem as though he's drunk."

It was a successful ploy. They left the house by the gate they had entered then turned into the road down to the town gate, all of them laughing and drinking from bottles and reeling as though drunk. Two of the men supported Galiano with his arms round their shoulders and pretended to be trying to give him another drink.

As they reached the gateway leading to the harbour they saw that there were now four guards there. The original two were in a drunken stupor, lying on the ground and snoring while the two new men, probably replacements were little better, leaning against the wall, each with a bottle. One of them roused himself as Andrews and his party approached and shouted to the man carrying the bundle of weapons, "What have you got hidden in there, something stolen eh?"

The seaman was ready and put his hand into the bundle to produce a bottle of wine. This he gave to the guard who looked at it stupidly before Humphries said in Spanish, "Good stuff that, share it with your mate". At this, the man grinned, knocked off the head of the bottle and took a long drink before waving the party on and out of the gateway where they turned and, still trying to look like a party of drunks, made their way to the beach and the boat.

Once they reached the beach Galiano was showing signs of coming to his senses so he was gagged again before being put into the boat. The two Indians were helping to lift him, speaking rapidly to each other in their native tongue when he suddenly grunted and convulsed. The Indians let him fall to the sand and then bolted out of sight. Andrews turned him over and found him bleeding from a wound in his side, obviously stabbed by one or both of the Indians.

"Wrap him in that canvas and into the boat with him, lively now," called Andrews.

The man was wrapped and all leapt aboard the boat. The seamen pulled as hard as they could back to the ship.

The first thing Andrews did once they were back aboard the *Eagle* was to call for the ship's surgeon to take a look at Don Galiano's wound by the light of lanterns. The man was still alive and moaning. After a quick inspection, Jameson shook his head and said that it was hopeless, the man was beyond help. Indeed, as they stood looking down on him, he convulsed again, tried to speak through his blood-filled throat and died.

"Don't blame yourself, Captain, it wasn't your fault. Those Indians were surely bent on revenge for what he had done to them and did what they felt that they had to do. We were taking him back to stand trial and almost certain execution so this is perhaps for the best" said Humphries quietly.

Andrews nodded. "Perhaps you are right, sir. At least we won't have a felon to guard day and night. Right, Doctor, have him made ready for burial at sea tomorrow." He turned to the men of the landing party who were clustered round the body. "Well done, you men. The plan worked perfectly apart from the murder of this man and you, Cartwright, that was quick thinking back there. Where did the bottle come from?"

"Off the table in the kitchen, sir," said Cartwright sheepishly. "Didn't seem that the prisoner would want it anymore. There were two, sir. I've got the other here and we took some of the food too. Sorry, sir."

"Don't apologise, man. You did well, but I'll keep my eye on you. Down to your quarters all of you, we have a busy day tomorrow."

Chapter Eighteen

Attack on Privateers' Vessels

At dawn the next morning, with the sunlight only faintly colouring the sky to the east, the men were at action stations as normal at dawn in King's ships. It was especially necessary as they were in what must be considered an enemy harbour, although the gun ports had not yet been opened. The town was quiet with few lights showing and nobody to be seen ashore.

"Still asleep, I should not wonder, Mr Davis," said Andrews when it became clear that there was no threat. "Dismiss the hands and let them have their breakfast. We'll sail after our own breakfast."

"Aye-aye, sir," replied the first lieutenant, turning away to give the orders.

One hour later the call, "All hands on deck to make sail", spoken in French for the benefit of the few small fishing boats that had appeared, brought the men on deck eager to leave Montevideo behind. The ship was pointing upstream due to the effect of the river current and there was a fair wind blowing offshore. Andrews looked round then gave the order, "Up anchor and make sail, jibs and tops'ls first if you please, Mr Davis, and have it done in a sloppy French way. Send up the Tricolour."

There were no incidents and with the men on the capstan bars straining to haul the ship up to the anchor against the current and with jibs and tops'ls ready but not sheeted in, the moment came when the shout from the foc's'l told the captain that the anchor was loose from the ground. Of course Andrews could see that for himself as the ship was already moving astern. Instantly the men hauled on the jib sheets to make the ship's head turn to larboard and then the tops'ls were sheeted home. Mr Firth, the master, was at the wheel with two of his mates and the ship began instantly to make headway upriver. There was plenty of room in the river for the inevitable tacking that would have to be done and Andrews was well satisfied. With a nod to the first lieutenant he asked that Mr Menzies the gunner should join him.

"Well, Mr Menzies, what progress have you made with the combustibles?"

"All ready, sir," was the reply, "but I may have to alter the powder charge a little depending on how close we are to our target. Don't want to shoot over 'em or into the sea. If I can use both our carronades as well as the cannon, sir, I will have different charges ready for both."

"Very well then, see to it. I plan to fire a larboard broadside into the Spanish warships but not including your combustibles as we pass, and then a broadside into the privateers this time including your stuff. Then we'll go about to give them the starboard broadside then go about again, another larboard broadside and then down river as fast as we can go. So you can use both carronades and two cannon each side to set fire to the targets. Instruct the gun captains carefully on what they have to do."

"Aye-aye, sir, I've picked 'em already."

Some miles upriver Andrews ordered the ship be anchored and all preparations be made for the attack in the morning. The officers knew exactly what was expected of them and instructed the gun crews again and again to be sure there would be no mistakes.

Andrews called the officers down to the great cabin to go over what he wanted. "I intend to have the ship off Montevideo as dawn breaks with enough light to let us see what is happening. The men will be at action stations with the guns loaded but not run out yet. We'll go down river under jibs and upper tops'ls and of course the flow of the river will help us. Mr Scott and Mr Duddy, remember that the gunner has his own orders and will fire separately to your broadsides. All clear, gentlemen? Good, then normal shipboard routine for the rest of the day, I want to see the ship cleaned and smartened up. This is a King's ship and it should look like it when we go into action tomorrow."

At the end of the middle watch, about four o'clock, with the ship ready in all respects, the anchor was raised and the ship moved down river. Andrews was concerned that he had not allowed enough for the speed of the current but his estimations had been confirmed by the sailing master so he could do no more but order the main upper tops'l to be furled. Dawn was breaking seemingly later than expected due to the low cloud which may herald a storm, but they arrived at Montevideo harbour exactly as anticipated. The King's colours were aloft and as one the gunports swung open. Andrews waited until the exact moment when the ship was opposite the Spanish ships, then ordered, "Open fire as your guns bear."

The guns on the larboard side spoke first in a full broadside including those two guns controlled by the gunner but as yet without the combustibles. Andrews keenly watched the results. The main broadside wreaked enormous damage to the ships with rigging torn and shot smashing through the hulls releasing lethal splinters which flew in all directions. Then they were past with the gun crews working frantically to reload. Andrews nodded to Lieutenant Davis who immediately bawled out the order, "Larboard battery ready to fire." He paused until *Eagle* neared the privateer ships then shouted, "Fire!"

This time the gunner's specially prepared cannon were included. Two of the combustibles landed on the decks of two privateer ships but one fell short.

"Stand by to go about." The current carried the ship well past the harbour before it was turned to head back. Again the gunner's weapons spoke, this time sending the combustibles across and onto the anchored ships before the starboard broadside fired. This time the target was partly obscured by the smoke from fires already burning but again the shot smashed home. Two ships were already sinking and as Andrews watched he saw masts and yards falling and flames rising from the decks of three others with the flames reaching over to the ships tied alongside.

Again the ship was brought round and a third broadside crashed into the privateers' ships but this time there was an explosion from for'ard. One of the gunner's cannon used for the combustibles had burst, scattering pieces of smashed gunmetal and flames across the deck accompanied by the screams of injured men. Other smaller explosions and screams followed as sparks landed on ready to use charges of gunpowder and set them off.

Andrews ordered all sail set and the ship headed downriver to the sea which was still many, many miles away. The strict training the men had undertaken paid dividends as the flames were rapidly extinguished, injured men were taken below to the surgeon, and dead men were dragged to the base of the foremast to be dealt with separately. The ship had not been fired on from the forts round the harbour and the only damage sustained was due to the exploded cannon.

Andrews stood on the quarter deck awaiting the reports from the gunner - if he was still alive - and the carpenter and bos'n on the state of the damage as well as from the surgeon on the wounded and dead. The first to report was the carpenter Mr Grinch. "Not too bad, sir. One gun is totally destroyed and another too badly damaged to be of any use. One carriage is too bad to repair, sir, and three others damaged but repairable. There is some damage to the side of the ship and to the deck above but that is easily repaired, sir, though it will take some time."

The next to report was the bos'n. "No damage on deck or aloft, sir. The ship is ready to face anything. Except a ship of the line, sir," he added.

The surgeon was next. "Sorry to have to tell you, sir, we have three men dead and seven badly wounded of which most will survive. The gunner is badly wounded but should be able to tell you what happened."

"Thank you, Mr Jameson, I'll come down." In the orlop deck, where the surgeon attended to the wounded men, he found the gunner slumped against the side of the ship nursing a broken arm. "How is he, Mr Jameson?" Andrews asked.

"Broken arm, sir, and one or two ribs as well, of course, as some burns but he will live. You can speak to him if you wish."

Andrews crouched down next to the man and touched him

gently. He opened his eyes and made to stand up. "Stay where you are, Mr Menzies, can you remember what happened?"

"Not clearly, sir. I was on the starboard side, sir, and a gun behind me exploded on the larboard side. I only know that because I've been told. How bad is it, sir, anybody killed?"

"Yes, there are three dead and seven wounded, I'm afraid, but the damage is repairable except for two of your guns. Now stay there and try and recollect what may have happened."

Back on deck, Andrews went for'ard and found a hive of activity as pieces of the smashed gun and the other severely damaged one were sent overboard. The carpenter and his mates were busy sawing wood to repair the damage to the decking and already patching up the hole where the gunport had been. The carpenter stood up and said, "I'm concentrating on the deck, sir, and the side. The weather looks bad and so I want to make us watertight first, sir, before looking at the carriages."

"Very good, Mr Grinch, let me know if you need anything."

"Aye-aye, sir," was the reply as Andrews turned to go back to the quarter deck where the first lieutenant was waiting to report. "How are we, Peter?" he asked.

"Not too bad, sir. You know about the damage and casualties I believe, but I don't yet know why it happened. We may not find out because three of that gun's crew were killed and the others severely wounded. Oh, and the only damage to the officers is young midshipman Peter Smith and Lieutenant Duddy. They were both on the gundeck amidships near the mainmast and received a knock or two on the head. Mr Jameson told them to go below."

Eagle was making rapid progress with her sailing qualities unimpaired, heading into the lowering clouds of an approaching gale. Astern there was no sign of any pursuit as the ship cleared the bay and then Punta Carreras perhaps because, Andrews mused, from what they had seen there wasn't a Spanish ship fit for sea and if one did follow them, the approaching gale would send it scurrying back to port.

Chapter Nineteen

Back at Sea

Out at sea, Merriman was waiting in a state of impatience for the return of *Eagle* and to know the results of Andrews' voyage up the River Plate. The two ships had weathered a gale which had moved inland and caused him concern for the *Eagle*. He couldn't help wishing that he could have gone himself but he did not need to be reminded that he was in command of the entire flotilla and must learn to delegate and to rely on others to carry out his orders.

Don't be such a fool, he scolded himself. *If anyone could be relied on it is David Andrews.* He paced up and down on the quarter deck, tugging at his ear as usual and with such a scowl on his face that nobody dared approach him.

Finally, on the afternoon of the eighth day, a sail was sighted and identified by Lieutenant Shrigley in the foretop with his telescope. "It's the *Eagle, s*ir. No doubt about it."

Soon the ship could be clearly seen from the deck and Merriman relaxed a little. He gave the order to heave-to but waited another minute or two before ordering the crew to stand down from action stations which he had ordered as soon as the sail was first sighted.

The *Eagle* rounded-to a hundred yards from the *Lord Stevenage,* drew up alongside and, brilliant seaman that he was, Andrews stopped his ship exactly parallel. His boat was in the water instantly and Andrews, wearing his best uniform, was soon climbing on deck to the salutes of the marines and the sound of the bos'n's mate's whistles. He was grinning all over his face as Merriman and the other officers welcomed him. Merriman, his impatience and bad temper now dispelled, took him and Humphries down to the great cabin.

"Peters," he shouted. "Where are you man?" He had barely got the words out before Peters appeared carrying a tray of glasses and bottles. When all were seated, Merriman asked, "How did it go, David? Did you see the Spanish warships and the privateer ships, and what about Don Galiano?"

"It's all in my written report, sir," said Andrews as he passed over a large wad of papers secured within a sealed envelope.

"Yes, yes, I know, but dammit man, tell me without the usual flamboyance the Admiralty requires in its reports," said Merriman eagerly.

"Yes, sir, well it all happened like this," and Andrews then related everything that had happened - the sight of the few Spanish ships unfit for sea service, the group of privateers anchored and tied together in twos and threes and finally the raiding party ashore and the result. "I'm sorry I couldn't bring Don Galiano back with me, sir, but he was killed." He told Merriman the rest of that sad event.

"I think that may be for the best, David. He would hang if we took him to Jamaica or any other of our bases and you have deprived the privateers of his well-organised plans for the future, not to mention that you have done severe damage to the warships. Tell me, how did you identify the privateer ships?"

"Oh, that was easy, sir. You remember the ship that followed us across the Atlantic, easily identified by its strange shaped Tops'ls? Well it was there, tied in the middle of the others and the sails were hanging to dry. Anyway Mr Humphries had also spoken to people ashore who told him."

"Good, carry on."

"Well, sir, early the next morning we took the ship upstream far enough to let the Spaniards think we had gone, then at dawn next day we returned and fired a broadside first into the Spanish ships and then attacked the privateers using the method you used on the plague ship in the Baltic and three broadsides. When we left one could see through the smoke and four of them were burning and others sinking, sir. Regrettably I lost four men because a cannon exploded and shattered; three were killed outright and another died later. So I had to carry out five burials at sea."

Merriman shook his head sadly.

"I tried to find out the cause but as I said four of the gun crew are dead and while the gunner was there, he was far enough away to only be wounded, although seriously. So he can only guess that one of the gun crew double charged the gun. It was one of the French guns that we captured with the ship, sir, maybe old and not really fit for service. We are now two guns short."

"An excellent report, but what about the Spanish ships?" asked Merriman.

"We'll have no trouble from them, sir. We saw only four. One of those had sunk at anchor and the others were not fit for sea, maybe their hulls are in as bad a state as the frigate we sank. Mr Humphries can tell you more because he went ashore."

Mr Humphries did so and Merriman eventually leaned back comfortably and said, "I think that completes the first part of our orders. We can return north to carry out the second part, don't you agree, Mr Humphries?"

"Indeed yes, sir, and glad I am to have done that."

"As am I, sir and now I suggest we return to Salvador to add to our stores. I am sure all ships will need fresh fruit and vegetables, maybe a pig or two, some live fowl and perhaps sugar, coffee and flour. So please have your lists of requirements ready for when we arrive there. David, I would like you to visit Captain Stewart on your way back to *Eagle* and inform him, with my compliments, what we are about to do."

Chapter Twenty

The French Frigate

The flotilla sailed north without seeing any other ships except small traders which they left alone. They arrived back at Salvador where, at the far end of the harbour, they found a French frigate at anchor.

"Shall we beat to quarters, sir?" asked Lieutenant Merryweather worriedly.

"Not as such, Henry, but we must be on our guard. Convention says that we cannot use a neutral harbour as a battleground, so let us hope that the French captain will adhere to that. But we will be prepared. I'll have the guns loaded but not run out, quietly now, no drums or shouting and normal duties for anchoring and sail handling will be done. Then have the men carry out their normal duties aboard. We shall ignore the Frenchman – for now."

As *Lord Stevenage* moved slowly to her anchoring point indicated by the harbour launch, she fired the required gun salute which was replied to by the guns in the fort. Merriman warily studied the other frigate through his glass and saw the French captain doing the same. *He might well be worried,* thought Merriman. *If it comes to it we outnumber him three to one but if he has only just come from France he may know of the proposed treaty. I'll wait and see.*

Down below, Merriman was changing into his best uniform to go ashore to see the governor when the marine sentry banged the butt of his musket on the deck and announced, "First Lieutenant, sir."

Merryweather entered with a look of surprise on his face. "There's a boat coming from the Frenchie with a flag of truce, sir."

"Right then, I'll come up, and please ask Mr Humphries to join me."

A small boat had been sent across and a lieutenant could be seen waving a white flag as it approached. "Find out what he wants if you will, Mr Humphries, but don't let him aboard." A stern warning to stand off resulted in the lieutenant waving a letter and shouting, "Lettre pour le capitan."

"Let him deliver it, Henry, but have a midshipman take it off him without him getting out of his boat."

The letter was a request from the French captain to come aboard to discuss important information. Merriman considered for only a moment then said, "Mr Humphries, please compose a letter in reply, in French if you will, and send an invitation to him to come over for dinner later at say, the first dog watch, four o'clock. And Mr Merryweather, I want everything ready by then to receive a captain with all due ceremony. Officers and men to be in their best clothes and the ship in tip top order."

Ashore Merriman and Humphries were met by the same non-English speaking Portuguese officer and taken to see the governor. He was delighted to hear of the death of Don Galiano and the destruction of his ships.

"Tell him, sir, that it will not be the end of privateering but there will surely be a lessening for some time to come, and you can tell him about the state of the Spanish ships too," said Merriman.

Humphries did so and after a brief exchange he said, "The governor hopes that you will not do anything warlike in his harbour with the French ship."

Having received confirmation of this - with the accepted proviso that they would defend themselves if attacked - the governor invited them to dinner the next day and told them that he had already asked the French captain and then let them go. They asked the carriage driver to take them to Captain McLeod's house where they were welcomed effusively by the captain and his wife.

"We saw your ships come in, sir. What brings you back, Captain Merriman, we had not expected to see you again?"

"Well, sir, I wanted to report to the governor and yourself what we have been doing." And he told McLeod what they had found out and what had been done.

"That is wonderful news, Captain. Perhaps we can continue to trade without fear of privateers, at least for the foreseeable future. Tell me, sir, is there anything else I can do for you?"

"Yes, there is, sir. How long has that French ship been here?"

"It only arrived in the last of the daylight last night, but it didn't fire the normal gun salute and as far as we know nobody has come ashore since."

"Captain McLeod, you will understand that most, if not all, of the crew of that ship are probably revolutionaries and will be violently opposed to anything that reminds them of the old regime in France. Given the opportunity, I believe they would happily smash statues and windows, even or maybe especially those in the cathedral or other churches. I further expect that they will want to visit the taverns and brothels in the lower part of town and will get roaring drunk if they have enough money, so I suggest that your soldiers should be alerted to that probability. I didn't think to tell the Governor so perhaps you will."

MacLeod nodded.

"Another thing, Captain, if they came all the way from France they may be short of supplies as we were. If you and your friends could refuse or at least be reluctant to supply them except at high prices they may give up and sail out to sea where my ships will be waiting for them. We have prepared lists of our needs as before and I would be pleased if you could arrange delivery today and tomorrow as we must leave at first light the following morning. And, Captain, this time I insist that we pay you."

"I will do so, sir, and I am sure that my fellow traders will be pleased to help. I'll send a message to the governor and soldiers will be prepared for trouble as they are when any ship arrives here. What I will do is to bolt and bar the doors of my warehouses and have a few men in each ready to defend them. My friends will likely do the same when I tell them although we and the soldiers cannot do anything else until provoked."

"Thank you, sir. My officers and myself have been invited to dinner with the governor tomorrow night and I understand the French will be given the same invitation, so perhaps I will see you there."

Later, all was ready on *Lord Stevenage* when a French boat, a bigger one this time, was seen putting off from the French ship. Once alongside the French captain climbed nimbly aboard with another officer and a civilian to be greeted by the full ceremony due to a visiting captain: the whistles of the bos'n's mates, the marines presenting arms and Merriman and the officers in full dress uniforms on the quarterdeck. The man looked keenly about him, raised his hat in response and announced, "I am Captain Jacques de Monte, sir, of the frigate *Le Tricolore* and I thank you for your invitation. This is my lieutenant, Henri Coignet, and the other gentleman is a representative of our government assembly, Citizen Magón. May we speak privately, Captain?"

"Indeed, Captain de Monte, but some of my officers must be present. There will be nothing that they cannot hear, I trust them all, sir."

In the great cabin Peters and Tomkins were waiting to serve drinks and the table was set for dinner, eight places in all.

"Captain de Monte, may I present my officers. This is my first lieutenant, Henry Merryweather, my second, Alfred Shrigley, and my fourth, De Mowbray. The other gentleman Mr Humphries is a representative of our government, here to see that I behave myself," said Merriman, trying to lighten the atmosphere.

There were a few dutiful smiles from the officers and then the Frenchman said, "Lieutenant De Mowbray, that sounds like a French name to me. Have you any French relatives, sir?"

"Yes, sir, somewhere. My father's name is from his family who fled France at the beginning of the revolution, but he had already met and married my mother, an English woman, years before and settled in England. I was born in England," replied De Mowbray. "And may I complement you on your spoken English, sir."

"Well, strangely enough, my grandmother was English. She

married a Frenchman a long time ago and settled in France. We could even be cousins because I think there was a De Mowbray connection somewhere."

They continued the conversation in French with Mr Humphries before Merriman coughed and asked them all to be seated. The meal consisted of roast pork and vegetables bought onshore that morning and, with the consumption of good food and plenty of wine, the conversation became more animated. Merriman had earlier told the officers to be careful what they said and he knew that on deck Lieutenant Bristow and the lookouts were watching for any movement from the other frigate and that most of his men were sleeping near their guns.

When the meal drew to a close and the plates were cleared away, Merriman said, "Mr De Mowbray, the toast."

"Yes, sir. Gentlemen, the King." All stood, even the Frenchmen, lifted their glasses and said, "The King."

Afterwards brandy was served, or wine if preferred, and then Merriman dismissed the servants, knocked on his glass for silence and said, "Gentlemen, now the reason for this dinner. Captain de Monte said in his letter that he wished to discuss something important - Captain?"

"Gentlemen, you may know that there have been talks between your government and French representatives of the First Consul of France, Napoleon Bonaparte, about a treaty. The preliminaries had been agreed and it only needs signatures on the final document for it to take effect, which should happen soon. I have here a document confirming this which I am to deliver to the Spanish in Buenos Aires. So you see, gentlemen, we may still be enemies but may be allies now. I would prefer to be allies and I will not attack you though I confess that some of my officers and men do not think the same way, so you should be on your guard at all times," said De Monte, shooting a wary glance at Citizen Magón who was glaring at him from across the table.

Merriman winked at Humphries and De Mowbray who began an animated discussion with Magón about the revolution, giving Merriman the chance to speak to De Monte.

"Thank you, Captain, for that information, do you think that you will be able to stop the hotheads on your ship taking any action?"

"Maybe not, sir. There are only a few I can rely upon. Most of them are keen revolutionaries so I cannot promise anything. I hope you will have realised that I am not a revolutionary, indeed I am from an aristocratic family and I can only save my head by taking orders as I am one of only the few capable captains left in the French navy after the guillotine was so busy. I think most of the men want to go pirating, after all they have not been paid for many months even before we left France."

"Captain, I know that his Excellency Governor Gilberto Escoveda has asked you to dinner tomorrow and he has invited us also. Perhaps then you could have the opportunity to tell us more."

"Possibly, but I am sure to have my minder from the French Government there also. I was able to come this evening because he wanted to see a British man-o-war."

"I see, Captain. It may be difficult to speak but you may be able to discreetly slip one of us a note?"

"I'll have to see, sir, but I tell you that if the men are determined on any aggression I will have no part in it and if my life is in danger I will have to do whatever is necessary." He stood. "Goodnight, gentlemen, we must take our leave."

When he had left with the usual ceremonies, Merriman called the officers back down to his cabin. "A strange situation. We may be enemies of the French or we may not but, as Captain De Monte reminded us, we must be on our guard against treachery. I don't think anything will happen until after the governor's dinner tomorrow night but who knows. I'll tell you that I have the impression that De Monte would happily sail away with us aboard this ship rather than stay with a mutinous crew where he may be killed. Now, our ships should finish loading tomorrow and be ready to sail so thank you, gentlemen, and good night."

Chapter Twenty-One

Lives Saved

As Merriman hoped, there was no overt action from the French ship except that some men and an officer went ashore presumably to look for supplies while another boat took a large group of men to the tavern area. To an outsider it would appear there were only normal shipboard activities on board. He summoned the captains from the other ships, told them what had happened and to expect the worst. Andrews said at once, "We have been at action stations all night, sir, discreetly of course. You can never tell what the damn revolutionary Frogs will do. Can't trust them."

"Surely there will be no trouble, sir?" said Stewart. "We are in a neutral port after all and I don't believe they will do anything. But, when I am back, I will have the men come to action stations, sir."

"Why are they not yet ready, Captain Stewart?" roared Merriman. "You are too gullible, sir. Never trust your enemy, be ready at all times for anything. Back to your ship, Captain, and go to action stations at once, but quietly, no shouting or drums do you hear? Now go."

After the man had left, Merriman turned to Andrews and said, "What can I do with him, David? He has no spirit and no ability to think for himself. His lack of thinking could easily get him and his crew killed. In short I wish he wasn't here but I can't just send him away on some flimsy excuse, it could ruin his career." He sighed. "Anyway, I have thoughts about this evening which I would like to share with you."

That evening, Merriman's boat, the cutter, rowed ashore with a full crew and weapons hidden in the bilge. Mr Humphries and Lieutenant De Mowbray were with him as well as six marines in full uniform with their Lieutenant Charles Goodwin. His cox'n Matthews was at the tiller. Andrews' boat arrived at almost the same moment. He had two officers and four marines and a sergeant with him, also with weapons concealed. They gathered together on the top of the harbour wall and Merriman checked once again that they all knew what to do or not to do. The governor's coach was waiting for them and the party was soon at the governor's residence where they were again welcomed by the governor and his wife. Other guests crowded round them clamouring for attention in a babble of different languages with Humphries doing his best to translate and answer.

Merriman spotted the French captain with two other French officers and a sullen-looking Magón at his side. The captain and officers were in full uniform but their companion was dressed plainly. He looked about himself at the glitter and sparkle with disgust clearly shown on his face. He was surely an ardent revolutionary. Merriman caught the captain's eye and nodded as did he.

When the meal was over, the governor gave a speech thanking Merriman and his officers for their destruction of the privateers' ships using extremely flowery language. To this Merriman simply replied that that was what they had been sent there to do and would be leaving the following day.

At that moment there was the sound of breaking glass from outside followed by the cracks of shots being fired, all easily heard through the open windows. There were sharp gasps from some of the guests who leapt to their feet with looks of concern on their faces.

A man in an officer's uniform appeared, walked quickly to the governor's side and whispered in his ear. The governor rose to his feet and banged on the table with the handle of a knife to attract attention. "Ladies and Gentlemen, please do not be alarmed. Some drunken men have been caught breaking windows and doing damage to the cathedral but they have been rounded up and are being taken to Fort Santa Antonia by our soldiers where they will be locked up."

Humphries translated for Merriman's benefit who replied,

"French sailors, I expect."

As the guests mingled after the meal, Merriman seized the opportunity for a word with Captain Macleod who told him that the French had been refused entry into the warehouses and that guards and soldiers had been placed ready for any problems. Merriman explained that he expected to sail early next day then he looked round for De Monte. He found him in deep conversation with his sullen companion and De Mowbray. Merriman nodded to Humphries who joined the group, skilfully putting himself and De Mowbray between the two Frenchmen to allow Merriman to get near to the captain. The two French officers were keeping themselves at a distance. The captains greeted one another cautiously, keeping their backs to the young Frenchman who was in a heated argument with the two Englishmen. De Monte carefully passed a small note to him and whispered, "That's it, Captain. Can you help us?"

Merriman moved away into a corner where he unfolded the note and read 'Sir, I am certain that we are to be killed tonight. My two officers are true. Can you help us?'

Merriman wandered back, took a glass of wine from a servant and made his way over to the governor. Passing the French captain he nodded slightly and whispered one word, "Wait". Then he made his farewells to the governor using the same excuse as the previous time and made his way back to his men and the French. There he beckoned to Humphries and asked him to tell the two French officers what they were to do. This done, Humphries turned and nodded to Merriman who said to the group, "It's hot in here. Shall we move nearer to the door? I can see a table there with untouched glasses of wine on it."

"Good idea, sir," said De Mowbray and, still arguing in fluent French with Magón about the French revolution, he began to move towards the door, slowly so as not to attract attention. The French captain grasped the idea immediately and he and his two officers crowded round the man who was so carried away with his argument that he didn't seem to realise what was happening until they passed outside.

The cool air seemed to sharpen his wits and he began to

complain until Merriman hit him on the head with an empty wine bottle he had snatched from a table. The man collapsed without a sound and the two French officers carried him out, down the steps and past the indolent sentries to where the governor's coach was waiting. Wasting no time, they had the coachman take them to the harbour but had hardly reached it before a French voice shouted, "Allo, where are you taking our officers?" A group of some six men gathered round the coach all bearing weapons. De Mowbray stood up and said in French, "Perhaps you should look behind you."

Taken completely by surprise, the men turned to see Merriman's ten marines and their officer with their fixed bayonets stood ready to use them. The French were quickly disarmed and Merriman said, "Right, Mr Goodwin, take them and this fellow Magón beyond the harbour and tie them up. If you can find their boat, set it adrift."

That did not take long and soon all of them were able to descend the steps to their boats which pushed off and rowed swiftly back to the *Lord Stevenage*. Once there, Merriman ordered Andrews to come aboard with him and send his own boat and the marines back to the *Eagle*. Once the Frenchmen were onboard, surrounded by suspicious marines, Merriman remarked, "That went well, David. Our plan worked. Don't you think so, Captain de Monte?"

The grateful man nodded and replied, "Indeed it did, sir. Thank you for saving our lives. My officers are grateful too but don't have much English to express it. But do I understand that you had planned it all in advance?"

"Indeed I did, sir, in the expectation that we might have to do something, but until I read your note we had decided to do nothing."

The night passed, the French were locked in a cabin with a marine on guard outside, and Merriman, after a few words with Andrews, sent him back to his ship. All three English ships were at action stations as dawn broke.

Chapter Twenty-Two

Destruction of a French frigate

The flotilla sailed at eight o'clock of the forenoon watch and sailed straight out to sea until the land was out of sight. Then, as previously agreed, they separated, Merriman to sail slowly south, Andrews to sail north and Stewart to stay in a position to see the French ship when it came out. All ships were to stay far enough offshore so that the coast was no more than a blur.

Merriman had ordered that all tops'ls be brailed up so as not to be easily seen by the French until too late, and yet ready to be set instantly. He expected that the French would head south, so the other two were to join him if they heard gunfire. It was Captain Stewart's task to determine which way the French ship sailed, either north or south it didn't matter, but to wait until the ship was well on its course and then fire broadsides from its small cannon to attract the others.

Merriman had gone south because he assumed that if the French ship was going from France to Buenos Aires it must go south. Nothing happened until mid-day when the sound of gunfire was heard. At the same time a lookout aloft with a telescope shouted, "Deck there, a ship. I think it's the Frenchie".

"Up you go, Mr Shrigley, and tell me what you see."

"Aye-aye, sir," was the reply and then the Lieutenant was climbing the shrouds like a monkey.

He could see clearly from the topmast and confirmed the lookout's report. A ship was sailing south, close to the coast. It must surely be the ship they were waiting for.

"Mr Merryweather, have the three French officers taken below and kept under guard and then beat to quarters if you please. Keep the tops'ls brailed up until we know he has seen us. The guns may be loaded with solid shot and run out. Mr

Henderson, we'll change course slowly to close with that ship, gradually now, and I'll have the boats over the side and streamed astern."

That was a wise precaution as lethal splinters would fly if the boats were smashed by cannon shot.

Above the noise of pounding feet, the squeal of the gun trucks and the roll of the marine's drums, were the sounds of banging and swearing below as men took down the cabin partitions and took those as well as chests and furniture to the hold. The lookout suddenly yelled, "Sail astern, sir, coming up fast. It's the *Eagle,* sir, and *Mayfly* also."

Impatiently Merriman climbed onto the lower mizzen ratlines to get a better look. It was the *Eagle* with all sail set racing along to join them with what sailors called 'a bone in her teeth ' referring to the large bow-wave she made.

"Mr Henderson, steer on a converging course with the Frenchman and Mr Merryweather, I'll have all sail set," ordered Merriman.

The topmen raced each other up and out onto the yards to the tops'ls and *Lord Stevenage* immediately surged ahead like the thoroughbred she was. Merriman knew he could do no more than close with the enemy and rely on his superior fire power to overwhelm it. His eyes scanned his ship, from the marines with their muskets in the fighting tops and behind the hammock nettings to the officers on the gun-deck, Mr Bristow and Midshipman Evans at the larboard guns and De Mowbray to starboard with Midshipman Small, all looking expectantly up to him, waiting for orders. Other men were ready to go aloft again to brail up the courses at the last minute. Nettings had been rigged overhead to catch any debris, or bodies, that might fall from aloft. *Eagle* was much closer and looked a brave sight with gun-ports open and the colours streaming out in the wind.

"Show our colours, Mr Green," Merriman ordered the signals midshipman, "and be smart about it."

"Aye-aye, sir," said the boy with a big grin on his face.

Soon Merriman could see that the French ship had crammed on as much sail as she could, trying to move ahead before the

Lord Stevenage closed to gunnery range but was too slow. Now Merriman could see the damned fellow Citizen Magón wearing a red revolutionary cap, waving his sword and shouting orders to the men, even pushing some into their positions. Nevertheless, *Le Tricolore* showed her teeth as the gunports opened, not all together as they should have done, but they opened and the black muzzles of her guns showed.

Merriman grinned at Merryweather and said, "I think we have her, Henry. We have her captain and two of her officers below so maybe they have only a sailing master and petty officers to handle her, but they will fight hard and with hatred I have no doubt. Keep your eyes on the weather coming up astern. We may have a gale to contend with before long."

It was true, heavy dark clouds were climbing into the sky and the wind was increasing from the north east. It would soon be necessary to shorten sail again. Indeed *Eagle,* coming up astern, but still at least two miles off, was already doing just that, her upper tops'ls disappearing like magic, but Merriman was determined to hold on until near the French ship.

It took only a few more minutes before he ordered tops'ls and courses furled and then the two ships were alongside separated by only two hundred yards of heaving, grey water. The French fired first, an uneven broadside as not all guns fired as one. In fact, one or two guns did not fire at all and most shot went overhead but a few thuds below could be felt before Merriman yelled, "Starboard battery, fire!"

The guns bellowed all at once and the men were already reloading before a reply came from the other frigate. This was where experience and training showed to advantage. The gun crews worked in the near darkness of billowing gun smoke, surrounded by the deafening noise of the guns and the shrieks of the wounded and the sound of cannonballs that penetrated the gundeck wreaking instant havoc to the sound of smashing, tearing wood and lethal flying splinters.

A reply came from the enemy, again not a regular broadside and *Lord Stevenage's* second broadside sounded like an echo of it so closely did it follow. In typical French fashion, most of their fire was directed at the masts, sails and rigging of Merriman's ship. Sharpshooters were firing from the mast heads of both ships and Merriman could feel the wind from several musket balls as he strode round the quarter deck, in fact splinters were sticking up from the deck planking to show where they had hit. The bos'n and his mates and topmen were desperately trying to repair the damage aloft, all the while exposed to the enemy's musketry which killed or wounded several of them.

Looking forward from the quarterdeck, Merriman could see some damage and many wounded men being dragged below to the tender mercies of McBride the surgeon. Even as he looked, a third broadside erupted from his ship and the enemy was hidden for a moment by thick smoke before the rising wind blew it away. Then he saw *Eagle* crossing behind him to fire her larboard guns into the stern of the French ship. The balls would crash along the full length of the gundeck, killing and maiming men and overturning some gun carriages on to wounded men lying on the deck. It would be the most damaging of the action this day.

Another broadside from *Lord Stevenage* crashed into the French ship to which there was little return fire and then another into her stern fired by *Eagle* from her starboard battery, gun by gun as each bore in turn, this time shattering the rudder stock. The smoke dissipated and the ship could be seen as a voice yelled, "She's on fire, sir".

It was so. Smoke could be seen amidships which quickly grew thicker and flames were seen. Merriman ordered Merryweather and Henderson, the master at the wheel with his mates, to bear away from it as fast as possible. No guns fired from the wreck and a wreck it was. The foremast was down and trailing alongside with men trapped in the tangle of rope, screaming and certain to drown.

Captain Andrews had taken his ship well clear and the two ships were now far enough away to be out of danger from the flames. The wind had increased which fanned the flames further and soon the ship was burning from stem to stern. Merryweather stood beside Merriman at the stern watching until the first lieutenant said, "Look, sir, she's drifting and is going to go ashore on those rocks."

The ship did indeed run aground, lifted high by the increasing swell and dropped like a small toy which then disintegrated in a massive explosion as her powder magazine ignited, throwing timbers, cannon, men and parts of men high into the air. The remains of the wreck continued to burn until it slipped off the rocks and sank in deep water.

"Well, that's the end of that, Henry. Can you see any men in the water needing rescue?" said Merriman.

"No, sir, not one," replied Merryweather, studying the wreck and the sea about it through a telescope.

"Right then, what is our damage and the how many men have we lost?"

The carpenter, the bos'n and the doctor were on the quarter deck to give their reports as Merryweather replied, "We have lost Mr Bristow, sir, as well as two master's mates and the marine lieutenant Goodwin, other marines and seamen, that I know."

"Thank you, and now I'll have the ship rigged for bad weather, you know what to do, and signal *Eagle* to move out to sea with us to avoid the lee shore," said Merriman as the three men reported what had happened in their own areas of responsibility.

The carpenter was first and he was happy to report that the hull was as sound as the day she was built. "Apart from an inch or two in the well, sir. The rest is mostly superficial damage, soon have it fixed, sir."

The bos'n was next. "A lot of rigging needs attention, sir, the French always did shoot high. I've got men working on it even now, sir."

"Very good, off you go while I hear the doctor's report."

"Could be worse, sir. There are seven dead including Mr Bristow, Lieutenant Goodwin and two master's mates. As for the wounded, only twelve, although I fear that two of them will not see another dawn. And I think you have been lucky, sir, judging by the holes in your trouser leg and your jacket."

Merriman looked down. There was a hole in his right trouser

leg and another in the loose unfastened jacket he wore. "Never felt a thing, Alan, but I was dashing about to make myself harder to hit."

The approaching gale was fierce but quickly blew itself out with no damage or complications. After the blow, Merriman signalled all ships to heave to and prepare the dead for the usual burial at sea. That grim business over, Merriman retired to his great cabin and called for the first lieutenant and Midshipman Gideon Small to join him.

"Now then, Mr Small, as you know we have lost Mr Bristow which means that Mr De Mowbray will now become Third Lieutenant and you will become Acting Fourth. My clerk Tomkins will do the necessary paperwork for you. You have been Acting Lieutenant before and I am certain that you are well capable of the duties that will fall to you. But remember that you are still the senior midshipman and you must keep the others under control and ensure they do their studies properly."

"Thank you, sir. I'll not let you down, sir," said Small.

"If I had any doubt, young man, I would not have promoted you and I will ensure that you take the examination for Lieutenant as soon as possible," said Merriman. "So take those white patches off your coat for the time being and go on deck and ask Mr Shrigley, with my compliments, to heave-to and signal the other ships to heave-to and the Captains to come here."

"Aye-aye, sir, and thank you again, sir," said the youth, leaving the cabin.

"The lad will do well, sir, I am sure of it," said Merryweather with a smile. "He is a competent seaman enough to stand watch even though he is only sixteen."

They continued with a discussion about the other officers and midshipmen while they waited for Andrews and Stewart to come aboard. "I have no complaints, sir, although our two newest midshipmen, Evans and Edwards, are slow to learn their lessons. The master has spoken to me about it."

"I'll speak to them about it later, Henry. When our two captains have left, have the French officers brought to my cabin."

Bumps alongside indicated that the captains had arrived and they were then ushered down to the great cabin. Merriman greeted them, offered drinks and then said, "Gentlemen, now that France has lost another warship, I'm pleased to say, and none of us have received serious damage, I propose to continue north to look for the wrecked Indiaman unless either of you have need of anything from Salvador?" Both men shook their head so he continued, "Very well, let us continue towards Salvador and at latitude ten degrees south we shall then have another council of war."

They left and almost immediately afterwards the sentry thumped his musket on the deck and shouted, "French officers and guards, sir."

"Send them in," Merriman replied, and then said, "Sit down, gentlemen. Peters, drinks for us here. Marines, wait outside."

When the drinks had been gratefully received, Merriman put on a serious face and said, "Gentlemen, you may be wondering why I called for you. You will have heard the gunfire and I must tell you that your ship *Le Tricolore* has been destroyed. She blew up and there were no survivors. I don't apologise for that, sir. You reported to me that treaty terms were being discussed back home but until confirmation of the signing of the treaty is reported to me, your ship was still my enemy. None of you had offered parole and so I had you confined below in case you attempted something against this ship."

"I'm sorry to hear that my ship - or what was once my ship - has been destroyed, sir, but in the circumstances I cannot blame you. There were still good men aboard but they were only few in number and completely dominated by that awful man Magón and his followers."

"Well, Captain, if you all give me your parole you will not be confined under guard any more, although there are certain areas of the ship which will be barred to you. I have been considering your future and I imagine that if I deliver you to some French possession in the Caribbean you might find it difficult to explain why you three officers were the only survivors from your ship. I imagine that your superiors in Paris may not be pleased. So I suggest you consider what would be best for you to do."

"Thank you, sir. I am grateful for your consideration. I agree with you that we might be in trouble with our superiors so we must think about it most carefully."

Chapter Twenty-Three

The Hunt for the Wreck

Weeks later, when they arrived at approximately ten degrees of latitude south, there was hardly any wind to carry them further. Merriman decided it was time a plan was thrashed out for the search for the wreck and he signalled for the captains to join him. He also called for Merryweather and the master to join them. When Peters had distributed drinks along with some peculiar Spanish biscuits, Merriman said, "Gentlemen, you know what we are here to do. Have you had any more thoughts about finding the wreck?"

"I have an idea," said Lieutenant Stewart. "My uncle sailed along this coast years ago when he was first mate aboard a small trading ship. He told me that the place is covered in tropical rainforest or jungle, except where Portuguese settlers have created small towns or villages, but from out at sea you could see small plantations of sugar and tobacco on the slopes of hills not far inland."

"Then, sir, if villages have been attacked and destroyed, we might still see traces of plantations," said Lieutenant Merryweather.

Merriman nodded. "Indeed we may, gentlemen, so this is what I propose. Now we are at the approximate latitude, we will sail directly westward until we sight land of Portuguese Brazil. Then I will sail northward while *Eagle* and *Mayfly* sail to the south for two days. If nothing is seen, I will sail south again and we will join forces and try further along the coast, but remember, the only charts of the coast that we have are the Portuguese ones, so when nearer to land we will reduce sail and proceed slowly with men taking soundings as we go. Any questions, gentlemen? No? Then let us be about it."

Two days later the cry, "Land ho! Starboard bow, sir," roused everybody. Suddenly men erupted from below and clambered up the rigging to get a better view. The officers gathered together on the quarterdeck, their telescopes busy. Merriman roared up to the lookout, "Can you see any ships of any kind?" A moment later the reply was, "No sail in sight, sir."

"Well, gentlemen, this is where our difficulties could begin. Mr Merryweather, we'll clear for action, load the guns but don't run them out yet and have our other ships signalled accordingly."

As they slowly approached the land, golden beaches could be seen in front of a wall of rainforest. Beyond this, the slopes of low hills or small mountains were visible but there was no sign of a river running into the sea. All ships had leadsmen in the fore-chains to ensure there was sufficient water beneath the keels and the brig was able to get closer inshore before they all anchored. Merriman called the two captains aboard for a brief conference.

"Gentlemen, as we decided earlier I will sail north for two days and if I find nothing I will sail south until I find you. You two will sail to the south for two days before turning back. It has occurred to me that where the tidal wave hit the shore and carried the ship inland, many trees will have been uprooted or smashed and carried inland as well. The forest will not have grown very tall again, so that could be a marker to look out for as well as plantations on the hills and a river. So, let us be about it."

The *Lord Stevenage* sailed up the coast but found nothing except some native people who stood at the edge of the rainforest in small groups, watching but not reacting or showing excitement at the sight of the ship. Even though Merriman ordered some of his crew to wave, there was no response. It was noted that the natives were all men, thin and wearing only a loincloth, and all were armed with spears and bows and arrows.

"'What are these, so withered and so wild in their attire that look not like the inhabitants of earth and yet are on it'," quoted De Mowbray.

"I see that you have been studying my Macbeth, Mr De Mowbray," responded Merriman." Well said, I cannot think of another suitable quotation."

"Not a very friendly lot are they, sir?" remarked Lieutenant Shrigley. "I wouldn't want to land there to meet them."

"No indeed, Alfred, but we are sure to have to go ashore eventually when we find what we are looking for and, if I am not very much mistaken, we shall have to follow a river up into the forest to find the wreck. Who knows what the native reaction will be."

At night the ship lay hove to with the men sleeping on deck at action stations with extra lookouts posted, but nothing happened.

After the two days, they turned south again but there was nothing to see, no ruined villages, rivers or inland plantations. On the third day they met the brig sailing north and an excited Stewart - at least as excited as was possible for the dour Scot - reported that they believed they had found the spot. *The Eagle* was anchored there waiting and Merriman had himself rowed over to *The Eagle* to find out what had been found.

"Well it looks very hopeful, sir," reported Captain Andrews. "As you can see, beyond the beach is a small stone fort and a few pitiful remains of a village. There is a river over there and up the river and behind the beach there is a mass of fallen trees and logs. Inland on the hills are what appears to be the overgrown remains of plantations with a few solitary ruined houses. Oh, and we have seen some decidedly unfriendly Indians."

"I agree, David, it does look hopeful, we must go ashore at first light tomorrow and explore. Mr Humphries has some trade goods which might render the natives somewhat friendlier. But if we can, the first thing to do ashore is to send water parties up the river to replenish our fresh water supplies. Nevertheless we would do well to remember that most of the towns along this coast have been attacked by the native people, especially the small settlements and villages, even the outskirts of the biggest towns, Salvador, Sao Paulo and Porto Alegre. Mr Macleod told me that most attacks were further in the past, but precautions must be taken."

Chapter Twenty-Four

Ashore and up River

As the pale light of dawn appeared in the east, the two biggest boats in the squadron rowed quietly to the beach below the remains of the fort. The first ran up on the sand and grounded. Marines were the first to land and they formed a defensive line with loaded muskets and fixed bayonets whilst Merriman and officers and seamen quickly followed. The second boat held fewer men but carried several water casks for refilling if good water was found and it stayed clear of the beach awaiting orders.

"Mr Humphries," called Merriman, "perhaps this is where you should leave some of your trade goods before we go up river to find good water."

Humphries rapidly laid out his goods on a spread cloth: tin basins, bigger cooking bowls and plates, some cheap jewellery and pieces of coloured cloth, all set above the high tide line. All men climbed back into the boat and both boats were then rowed up to the river mouth, conscious of the curious faces of native Indians looking out from behind the shelter of the trees. A little way up the river they came to a point where the salt water of the sea became first brackish and then to a point where the water was clean and potable. No natives were to be seen there.

"Right then, Lieutenant De Mowbray, you will stay here with most of the men. The marines with their sergeant will form guard and the men will scrub out those casks and refill them whilst I go back to the ship. I will send more boats with empty water casks to be filled and you can arrange a shuttle service out to the ships."

"Aye-aye, sir," responded the Lieutenant cheerfully. "We'll work as fast as possible."

Rowed out to the two smaller ships, Merriman called at each

to tell the officers to have their empty casks taken to the river for filling and to keep a fast shuttle service going. The brig with its shallower draught was anchored nearest the beach and Merriman ordered Lieutenant Stewart to keep guns loaded and ready in case of trouble ashore. Soon boats were going backwards and forward and full casks were being hoisted aboard, a satisfactory sight to Merriman as replenishment with good fresh water was a priority for ships on extended voyages. Indeed most of the water still aboard had already developed a slime which had to be scrubbed out of the casks with sand.

There was no more sign of native Indians but at some point it was noticed that the trade goods left on the beach had disappeared. Merriman decided to go ashore again, leave some more trade goods, and then visit the fort. He left his first lieutenant in charge of the *Lord Stevenage* with orders to keep the remaining men at action stations and to keep a keen look out.

"Don't want to be caught with half our men ashore, do we, Mr Merryweather? I will take the remaining marines and go ashore again to investigate the fort."

With the marines under the command of Captain St James and with a few armed seamen, they trudged up the beach through deep soft sand and round to the rear of the fort. The men chattered excitedly about being on shore again and were looking around them at the encroaching rainforest. It was obvious that the fort had been badly damaged by the huge tidal wave. The upper and thinner part of the walls had completely disappeared leaving only the thicker part remaining standing little higher than six feet or so. The gates had gone and there was no sign of any structures which may have been inside; it had been swept clean.

The village was no better. Wooden buildings had been swept away leaving only the base and foundation of a small stone-built building. There was no life to be seen but one of the marines pointed to what had been a water well, surrounded by a low stone wall which had survived.

"Full of sand, sir, will have to be dug out again if we are to use it," reported Captain St James.

"Very well, Edward, there is nothing we can do here. We can go and see how the watering is going, but does that gap in the trees over there look to you as if it might have been a road going uphill, perhaps to the plantations?"

"Yes, sir, it may be, but from what we could see from the ship as we approached, the plantations are overgrown. It is unlikely we will find any of the villagers up there. Indeed, didn't Mr Humphries tell us that the one survivor of that doomed ship had said that his party had been attacked by the natives here and men killed?"

The watering was being well organised and the sweating seamen were busy scrubbing the insides of the casks while others filled them and rolled them down to the boats. A constant stream of boats was travelling between the shore and the ships and a coatless lieutenant was urging the men on to greater efforts, in fact some of the marines were helping, leaving only half of them on guard.

"How is it going Mr De Mowbray?" asked Merriman.

"Tolerably well, sir. The men are working well and I think they are enjoying themselves in these surroundings. I believe that *Mayfly* is almost finished and I have set their boats to join the others taking water out to the other ships. They aren't full but they have a good fresh supply already."

"Well done, Lieutenant, but we must continue whilst there is daylight. Send word that the most exhausted men are to be replaced by the men still on the ships who have only been watching."

"Aye-aye, sir," De Mowbray replied.

Watering continued until it was too dark to see by which time the ships were abundantly supplied. Merriman was well pleased and called the other two captains and Humphries to join him in his cabin for dinner.

"I'm sorry that I have nothing better to offer you, gentlemen, little more than ship's fare. As you know most of our fresh food was finished days ago but there is still one miserable goose which I have had the cook prepare for us. Most of the others drowned in the last gale. I can offer you a fairly good brandy afterwards. Captain Andrews, Mr Humphries?"

"Yes, sir, that I would enjoy," they chorused as one.

"Captain Stewart, what do you say?"

"No, sir," the man replied. "I will touch neither spirits nor any form of alcohol. I was strictly brought up by my stern Scottish father who condemned it from the pulpit as the invention of the devil. He used to say, 'Why should men put an enemy in their mouths to steal away their brains?' I believe that is a quotation from Shakespeare's Othello. I apologise, sir, but don't let it stop you enjoying it. I cannot change the habit of a lifetime but as far as ship's fare, I am well used to poor rations, my family in Scotland had a hard time to survive which is why I went to sea."

"Well, Captain Stewart, I think you are missing one of the good things of life but each to his own. I will not try and change you. I didn't know that you were a reader of Shakespeare. Mr Grahame, whom you did not meet, was also and we used to amuse ourselves and try and score points by finding suitable quotations. Now, gentlemen, to business. We have our water supplies replenished and I think that tomorrow we must proceed with the other part of our mission. I want you, David, to take your ship well off shore to keep your eyes open for the frigate you saw or indeed any other that may be about. Small ships you can try to catch and see what you can learn about Spanish and French activities, but do not attempt to tackle anything big. Come back and inform me of anything you see if it is likely to be a threat to us."

Merriman paused for a moment to collect his thoughts then continued, "Whilst you are taking the part of guard dog, David, Lieutenant Stewart and myself will pursue our main purpose which is of course the recovery of the all-important chest from the wreck. This is what I propose. I will go upriver in the longboat with armed seamen and marines to see if we can find the wreck. It is possible that the river will become too shallow further inland for the boat to float in which case we shall have to depend on our own feet which won't be easy."

"Indeed not, sir," said Stewart. "My uncle spoke about it.

Apart from the trees, there is thick undergrowth which will have to be cut to form a path. There are all sorts of stinging and biting insects and the place could be alive with poisonous snakes. Nevertheless, sir, I am prepared to volunteer to lead the shore party."

"Thank you for that, Lieutenant, but I need you to take your ship up to and as close to the river mouth as possible and watch where we go. If we have trouble with the natives I will have a red rocket fired and it will be your duty to fire cannon shot into the forest either side of the river which may discourage any further trouble. So keep your lookouts alert. There is one other thing I want you to do if necessary. If *Eagle* appears signalling a warning, you must fire three closely spaced cannon shots to let me know. I will leave my ship further out from you to be able to relay any signals to you. Mr Merryweather will be in command of her with Lieutenant Shrigley. Is all that clear?"

"Aye-aye, sir," they replied together.

"Of course I must go with you in the boat, Captain," said Humphries.

"Indeed you will not, sir," replied Merriman. "We don't know what we may find up that river. There may be trouble with natives and in any event we may not even find the wreck. I insist that you stay here."

"But, sir, I know what we are looking for, it is my responsibility, I must go," argued Humphries.

"And you are my responsibility, sir. What will happen to your responsibility if you are killed by natives or bitten by a poisonous snake and die of it? I cannot allow it."

After the others had left, Merriman called his own officers down to tell them what he had planned. "I'll take two boats, both manned by sailors and marines but the second to stand by in the river to act as a guard boat and help if necessary. Acting Lieutenant Small will be in charge of that one with Midshipman Evans. I will take Lieutenant De Mowbray and Midshipman Edwards and my cox'n Matthews with me in the first boat. All men to be armed and we will have a swivel cannon in the bows of each boat loaded and ready. Food and water and extra ammunition will be carried. We will start at first light tomorrow."

Chapter Twenty-Five

Discovery of the Ship, Indians Attack

Dawn was only just showing over the eastern horizon when the two boats quietly entered the river. All the men not rowing were keenly watching the dark forest on either side with their weapons at the ready.

"Do you think we really will have trouble with the natives, sir?" asked Midshipman Edwards in a whisper.

"Well I hope not but we cannot be too careful, Mr Edwards, so we must be alert."

The boats continued around a bend of the river and even further before Merriman called to the second boat to stop and anchor whilst he continued up stream. As had been predicted, there were few large trees still standing but smaller ones were sprouting vigorously between the fallen trunks and the undergrowth was so thick it looked to be almost impenetrable. Some five hundred yards further, the boat grounded briefly but was cleared of the obstruction by men using their oars as poles to push the boat onwards. The river was narrowing and as a result the flow of water increased and the oarsmen had to pull harder to make progress. There was a lot of noise from the forest. Screeching troops of monkeys were loud from high in the trees and the calls of alarmed birds responded.

"Sir, I think I can see the stern of a ship, sir," called a seaman by the gun for'ard. "It's well ahead and almost covered in growth, sir, but it looks like it. Up that side channel, sir."

"Well done, Jackson. Mathews steer for it."

It was indeed the wreck of a ship, stern on to them and tilted high into the air. What they could see through a tangle of vegetation was that the windows of the great cabin had been stove in, the rudder had disappeared and there was no sign of any deck railings. Some ropes trailed forlornly over the side but were doubtless rotten by now. The short side channel rapidly shallowed and the boat slowly came to a halt because the wreck was surrounded by wet marshy ground full of rotting vegetation making further progress by boat impossible.

"It seems that we shall have to do this the hard way then," said Merriman. "Mr De Mowbray, you will stay here whilst I and some men try to walk or wade through this mess. Matthews, Jackson and you two men, Gibbins and Owens, come with me and Matthews, you bring your flint and steel and a piece of burning slow match with you. Jackson, sling that coil of rope over your shoulder. All of you bring your pistols and cutlasses."

They dropped over the side and slowly struggled towards the wreck through the morass, sometimes only ankle deep and other times up to their knees. There was no hope of boarding the wreck at the stern so they had to struggle forward to where the remains of the ship disappeared down into mud and vegetation. They were nearly there when Merriman shouted at them to stop and not move as some small snakes appeared in front of them then crawled and half swam away.

When they reached a point that offered a reasonable chance of boarding the wreck, Merriman said, "I'll go first if some of you help me up, then I can drag the rest of you up, but be careful where you put your feet. The deck timbers may be rotten and we must be aware of snakes."

Once aboard, the five men stood in a group and looked around them. Suddenly the men began to swear violently and dropped their trousers revealing black leeches clinging to their legs and buttocks. "Filthy bastard things," shouted one of the seamen and Merriman was quick to act.

"Don't pull them off," he shouted. "That is the last thing you should do. Matthews bring the slow match here."

Merriman's party immediately began to clear leeches from their legs with the slow match, blowing on and then touching the glowing end to the leeches. Soon the men were free of the things which dropped off and disappeared back into the water.

"Keep that slow match burning, Matthews, we will doubtless

need it when we go back to the boat," said Merriman. "Now follow me."

They inched their way slowly up the slope of the deck towards the stern of the wreck. The only incident was when Merriman put his foot through a piece of rotten timber. Approaching where the cabins had been, they saw that all the partitions had been swept away by the giant tidal wave and they found only pieces of shattered timber and a few fittings still clinging on, strangely enough including a lantern with shattered glass. Jackson shook it and said, "Still oil in this, sir."

Right at the stern of the ship they came to what had been the captain's cabin. There was nothing left inside. Again, the main partitions and doors had gone but beneath the shattered stern windows, Merriman could see that the lockers seemed to be intact although shrouded with creeping vegetation which was growing through the empty window spaces. He moved towards them but a stirring in the shadows to the side of the lockers warned him of a threat and he backed away.

"Jackson, bring that lamp and see if you can light the wick with the slow match so we can see what is in that corner."

The wick caught fire instantly and the sudden bright light revealed a large snake coiled there regarding them with suspicion.

"Well it may be poisonous or it may not but there is only one thing we can do. We must kill it before it can attack us," said Merriman drawing a pistol from his belt and cocking it. "If we all shoot together and aim for its head, at least one of us should hit it." The men all pulled pistols from their belts and cocked them. "All ready men? Alright then, fire!"

The roar of the pistols in the confined space was deafening and the flash and the powder smoke almost blinded them but as it cleared they could see the creature writhing and twisting about in the corner. Two pistol balls had hit it in the head and it was dying. Merriman stepped towards it and cut off the remains of the head with his sword. They all looked down at the remains and gasped at the size of it. "Must be near eight feet or longer, sir," said Jackson. He moved the head with the tip of his cutlass and said, "Look, sir, I don't think it was poisonous, it doesn't have big fangs. I think it killed its prey by coiling round it and squeezing it to death."

"You may be right, Jackson, it may be a python. Such snakes devour their prey whole. Look at that bulge in its middle. Probably its last meal still being digested. Maybe a careless monkey or small deer or some such. Those of you who were with me on our trip to India must have seen pythons there."

"Aye, sir, and nasty big things they are. Many snakes there are very poisonous especially cobras and kraits, I hate the crawling things, sir," said Matthews.

"Well, that's one snake that can do us no harm now, Matthews, so now we must try and get into those lockers. In case any of you don't know what we are looking for, it is a small stoutly built chest containing important documents from India."

"Aye, and treasure too," muttered Gibbins, one of the two seamen.

"What did you say, Gibbins?" asked Merriman.

"He said treasure, sir," Matthews said. "It's all over the ship, sir, we all know."

Merriman shook his head and smiled mirthlessly. He should have known. A secret could not remain a secret for long in the crowded conditions aboard ship. The marine guard outside his cabin could have heard what was spoken about or a man on the quarterdeck could have heard through the open skylight.

A hail from Lieutenant De Mowbray in the boat asking if all was well distracted him from musing on this further.

"We are fine, Lieutenant, it was only a snake and I think we may have found the chest," he shouted back.

He turned back to the men and said, "You are all a lot of gossip-mongers and you can tell everybody I said so. Now, get that plant growth cleared away and those lockers open, but watch out for snakes and such things."

Strangely two of the three lockers opened easily revealing only mildewed and rotting clothing and bedding. The third was more difficult having been locked, but it soon yielded to heavy blows from a cutlass which split the door open. They all crowded round to see what was revealed. It was indeed a small brass-bound chest with two heavy padlocks. Also inside the locker were two rusted pistols and a fine sword, this only slightly rusted having been wrapped in an oiled cloth.

"Must have been the captain's sword so we'll take it with us. His family might like to have it. That's it, men, now we have to get it down to the boat." Merriman thought for a moment then said, "Matthews, tie the rope round it and secure it properly, then we can hang it out of the stern window and collect it on the way back to the boat. That would be easier than trying to carry it all the way."

"Aye-aye, sir," he replied eagerly, securing the chest in a cradle of knotted rope leaving plenty of spare length. The two seamen lifted it up onto the mildewed window ledge and began to lower it down the stern of the wreck. Merriman watched carefully. "Handsomely now, don't let it get into the water again. Now belay it to that beam above you."

As the men turned away from the window to follow this order, one of them, a man by the name of Gibbins, fell to the deck choking on an arrow through his throat.

Almost immediately there followed a volley of musketry from the boat below and a shout from Lieutenant De Mowbray. "There are a lot of the natives, sir, and they don't seem to like what you are doing. They have shot arrows into us here in the boat as well as shooting at you. I have two men injured. Can you get back quickly, sir? We shall have to move."

Merriman risked a quick peep out, saw the men in the boat reloading their muskets and shouted down, "Which side are they shooting from, Lieutenant?"

"Starboard side, sir. We've seen them there but none on the larboard side, at least we haven't seen any."

"Very well, use the swivel gun if you need to. We will come back to you on the larboard side of the wreck. Have your men ready to give us covering fire when we cut that chest down and wade back to you."

"Sir, you won't be able to reach the chest, it is too high up and the rope isn't long enough."

"Right, men, we'll have to pull the chest back and leave it here with Gibbins. Poor Gibbins is dead so we shall have to leave him as we can't carry him back with us through that mess below us. So, men, make sure that your pistols are reloaded and we are ready to go."

Carefully the four of them moved down to where they had climbed onto the wreck and began to move along in the cover of the hulk until their next move would be into the open. Merriman risked a glance out to see the men crouched in the boat with muskets at the ready. Even as he looked, half the men fired and dropped back to reload. Obviously De Mowbray had organised the men into two parties because then the second group of men rose and fired before the swivel gun spoke and a hail of shot peppered the trees. The first men, having reloaded, poked their muskets over the gunwale of the boat ready to shoot again at anything moving.

"The best time might be now, sir," yelled the lieutenant.

Merriman immediately ordered his three men to move out to the boat and he followed behind. No more arrows came from the forest and they reached the boat safely and climbed aboard. The boat was floating free as the lieutenant, in the time before the attack, had turned it round ready. Men were ready to thrust the oars out and pull as hard as they could down river again. Merriman and his small party immediately set about getting rid of leeches with the slow match and then Matthews took his rightful place at the tiller. After all he was still the cox'n of the captain's boat.

As they approached the bend in the river, the second boat appeared with the men pulling madly at the oars and the marines crouched with muskets at the ready. At the sight of Merriman's boat, the men stopped rowing and a very relieved Lieutenant Small welcomed Merriman alongside.

"Glad to see you, sir. We thought we heard musket fire but we couldn't hear properly because of the noise from the forest so I had the men pull slowly up river but then we heard the cannon and knew there must be trouble and we came as fast as we could."

"Thank you, Lieutenant. We lost one man dead and two wounded, so back to the ship at once," said an exhausted Merriman.

Once back aboard, the two wounded men were handed over to the ship's surgeon. Doctor McBride assessed them then said quietly to Merriman, "I can't do anything for the man with the arrow in his belly, sir, although I will try, but the other man should be fine as long as no infection sets in. Many of you seem to have been bitten by flying insects but I have something that will stop the need to scratch."

"I know you will do your best, Mr McBride." Merriman turned to Merryweather, the first lieutenant, who was grinning all over his face. "Anything to report, Henry? No sign of *The Eagle* yet?"

"No, sir, nothing unusual except that we have seen a lot more natives in the trees behind the beach."

"Very good. Please see to it that the boat crews have a tot of rum and have the doctor see to the legs of those that were attacked by leeches. Now I'm going below to wash and change and have a drink of something stronger than water. Peters, where are you man?" he shouted.

"Right behind you, sir," was the reply and Merriman turned to see his servant standing there with a glass of brandy in his hand which he offered to his captain.

"Oh, good man, I need that," said Merriman, downing the brandy in a gulp. "Now then, below with you, I'm going to need a wash and change and then the doctor can look at my wounds. After that you might find me something to eat."

Later, washed, shaved, changed and fed, he sat back contentedly in his chair and considered his next move.

The marine sentry outside the cabin banged his musket on the deck and called, "Doctor McBride and Mr Humphries to see you, sir." The two men entered, the doctor carrying a small bag and Humphries nearly bursting with excitement.

"What did you find, Captain, what did you find?"

"All in good time, sir, all in good time. You must allow the good doctor to examine my legs which attracted the attention of some blood sucking leeches." He pulled up his trouser legs and McBride examined his legs.

"Hmm, hmm, very good. You should have no trouble, sir. Leeches can leave their teeth sticking into a wound if they are pulled off but you didn't pull the damned things off. I understand you had the foresight to use a slow match, so all should be well, but I have a salve to rub on to be sure. I have seen to your other men."

"Thank you, Alan. How are the injured men?"

"I'm sorry, sir, the one man died but the other with the arrow in his shoulder will recover. I extracted the arrow easily."

"Good. Now then, Mr Humphries. I know you desperately want to know what happened so I will tell you." Merriman related all that had happened and ended by saying, "So you see, the chest is there and we shall have to go up the river again but next time I shall see to it that we are better equipped for what we know is up there."

"What other preparations can you make, sir, and will you let me go with you next time?"

"No, sir, I will not. And, gentlemen, be so kind to pass the word with my compliments for Lieutenant Merryweather and Mr Green, the ship's carpenter, and Mr Brockle the bos'n and my cox'n Matthews to come to my cabin to discuss my plans for our next move up river."

Chapter Twenty-Six

Second Try to Rescue the Crate

In his cabin Merriman eyed the three men gravely. He asked if they had heard of mantlets. They all looked at each other and the carpenter said, "Mantlets, sir, 'aven't 'eard of 'em before. Are they some kind of French sailors like matelots, sir?"

Merriman laughed. "No, they are screens of a kind, made of wood to protect archers in the old castles. What I want you to do, Mr Green, is to construct some for the boats. Here, I'll show you what I mean."

He had pen, ink and paper ready and he drew diagrams for all to see and understand. "They must be at least high enough to protect the men at the oars and with pieces cut out to allow the oars to be used. They will also provide some protection for the marines and men with muskets who can shoot over them. Space must be left at the bows to allow for movement of the swivel gun. Have you suitable wood in your stores to make them, Mr Green? Remember we don't want them to be too heavy, and try to make two or three small shields a man can carry."

"Aye, sir, I think I have suitable wood. May have to raid Mr Brockle's stores too, sir."

"Right then. You can make a start right away. We will use the same two boats as last time. Have the boats brought on board if you need to. I will come up to inspect your efforts in good time. Mr Brockle, I want you to prepare the things we will need on my boat." He ticked them off on his fingers. "Longer rope than we had last time - at least half as long again - and another thinner one of similar length, six bottles of lamp oil, a small keg of powder and an extra length of slow match, a small cannon ball in a string bag, a well-greased snatch block and ask the sailmaker for a piece of canvas to wrap a body in. Only the one boat will need all those but ensure that each boat has enough powder and shot for the swivels and each seaman to have pistols and swords. The marines will bring their own weapons. Is that clear?"

"Aye-aye, sir," they chorused and left.

Late that afternoon, a breeze sprang up and as the sun began to set, Merriman called for the marine officer Captain St James.

"Edward, we have been neglecting our sword play of late and I think that you should begin your classes again."

St James was an excellent swordsman and he and Merriman had spent a few hours each day on deck practicing to improve Merriman's use of the weapon. There was little that the marine could do now to actually improve Merriman's skill but the practice was always beneficial. The other officers also had benefitted from St James' expertise and Lieutenant De Mowbray, who was already a skilful swordsman, helped in the teaching. Once the ship had come higher into the tropics though, the practice had almost ceased due to the heat.

They continued until it was almost too dark to see before Merriman said, "Edward, I feel better for that. It does no harm to sharpen one's wits, does it? I think that it would be a good thing if you would restart your lessons with the other officers, at the coolest part of the day of course. We are likely to meet Spanish or French men-of-war in this area and we may have to fight."

The next morning, at first light, the two boats proceeded slowly up river. This time they looked totally different than on the previous day. They looked like great beetles with oars for legs. Mr Green had done a fine job of the mantling, the weight of which made the boats ride visibly a little lower in the water. They proceeded with no interference from the native Indians until they reached the wreck. It was not until the boat stopped and Merriman, with four men each carrying part of the extra items, climbed out and began the slog through the mud and rotting vegetation that the first arrows arrived. They came from the starboard side as before but three of the men held the crude shields made by the carpenter and nobody was hit. Nothing of the natives could be seen as the heavy foliage concealed them and Lieutenant De Mowbray wisely kept his marines hidden ready to stand and shoot the moment an enemy could be seen.

Merriman and his four men reached the place where they had boarded the wreck last time and they were quickly aboard.

"Now then, Matthews, pass along that slow match and all of you drop your trousers and get rid of these leeches. Remember they must not be pulled off."

Once that unpleasant task had been done, they moved into the remains of the captain's cabin. The new men swore at the sight of Gibbins lying there dead with flies and maggots all over his face and they gasped at the size of the enormous dead snake in the corner.

"You two men wrap Gibbins in that canvas we brought and put him to one side. Which of all of you men is the best at heaving the lead?"

The men looked at each other and finally Jackson said that he thought he was.

"Right then, Jackson, take the longest rope and tie it to the net with the small cannon ball in it then secure the other end to that beam above you."

Jackson did as he was told and then stood waiting for the next order.

"Do you think that you can throw that ball far enough to reach our boat without showing yourself at the window more than briefly?" asked Merriman.

The man took a quick look and said, "Oh aye, sir, won't be difficult." He took a moment or two to make sure that the rope would pay out easily, then standing well back from the smashed window space, he swung the weight round and round a few times and released it. It went out straight and true and a hail from the men waiting in the boat told them that they had it safely on board and secured.

"Well done, Jackson," said Merriman. "Now put the snatch block on it and secure the other piece of rope to that, then two of you can lift that chest and carefully hook it onto the block.

When all was ready he shouted, "Lieutenant, are you ready?" De Mowbray, who had been told what to expect, shouted back, "Ready, sir, send it down."

The two men who had been holding the chest back released it and it began to travel easily down the rope held back only by the rope controlled by Jackson. He paid it out slowly until a hail from the boat told them that the chest had arrived and been placed in the bottom of the boat. During those few minutes the natives shot many arrows at the window and at the chest but, thanks to Merriman keeping his men away from the window, nobody was hit, although the chest arrived at the boat with some arrows sticking in it.

The men then looked to Merriman and Matthews asked what they were to do with the body of Gibbins.

"I had originally thought that we might send it down like the chest, but it will be unwieldy and when it reaches the boat men may be killed or wounded if they expose themselves to lift it aboard. The weight will make the rope sag more and the body will likely be in the water. No, we'll give Gibbins a Viking's funeral."

"What's that, sir>" asked one of the men.

Merriman knew that the mostly unlettered sailors put great store in giving a dead crewmate a solemn funeral at sea, so he replied, "It is like a state funeral given to a dead Viking warrior, a high honour. The dead man is put aboard a longboat with oil and wood and pushed off from shore. Then burning arrows are fired into the boat to ignite a fire. It is a great honour as I said and I think Gibbins would approve. What do you think?"

"Yes, sir," said several of them excitedly but then faces fell as a man said, "But we haven't got a boat to spare, sir."

"No we don't, but we have something bigger. This ship. We have brought oil and that small keg of powder and a slow match so we can make this old wreck into a fine funeral pyre. Agreed?"

"Aye-aye, sir. It's a fine idea," said Matthews.

"Good, then put Gibbins in the centre of the deck with that snake at his feet like the Vikings did with the body of an enemy and pour the oil all round him, then place the keg in the middle and set a fuse of slow match, say twenty minutes to give us time to get back to the boat and get some distance away. Then you can cast off that rope, the other boat can take it in. This deck timber and the deckhead are all dry and should make a big fire. Matthews, you set the fuse and we'll leave. But first I will say the words that I can remember from the funeral service."

The men stood silently with heads bowed as Merriman said the few words, then Matthews lit the fuse and they moved down the deck and slid into the mud and mess and waded to the stern of the wreck. Merriman shouted to Lieutenant De Mowbray to give covering fire as they waded back to the boat and the marines rose and emptied their muskets into the forest. A moment later, the swivel gun sent its charge of shot into the foliage and the second party of marines fired. By then Merriman and his men were safely aboard and busy with getting rid of the leeches from their legs.

"Pull away to a safe distance, Lieutenant, we'll wait. We have set a fire and there will be an explosion soon."

They did not have long to wait. First came the boom of the powder exploding and shortly after flames could be seen rising and greedily attacking the wood. Soon the entire stern of the wreck was fiercely ablaze, the heat making outer timbers steam as dampness evaporated. The men stared fascinated until Merriman said, "Time to go back to the ship I think, Lieutenant."

"Aye-aye, sir," was the reply and the men were soon rowing lustily to take the boat downstream.

Back aboard his frigate at midday, Merriman looked down at the boat and was surprised to see how many arrows were sticking out of the mantlets. They had done what was expected of them and not a single man had been hurt.

"Welcome back, sir," exclaimed Merryweather. "Glad to see you all safe and sound. Those mantlets seemed to work."

"Yes, they did, Henry. I know the carpenter wants his timber saved but tell him to take them off and keep them somewhere. We might need them again sometime."

All the officers and Mr Humphries were gathered round to see the chest and Humphries said, "You got it, sir, you got it, can we open it?" He was clearly itching to get his hands on the contents.

"Not yet, sir. Captain St James, we haven't got keys for these locks so have your marines shoot them off while we all stand clear."

But before the marine could give the order a hail from the lookout aloft was heard, "The *Eagle* coming, sir. She's flying a signal but I can't make it out"

"Belay that order, Mr St James. Have two of your marines take the chest down below to the orlop and stand guard on it. Mr Green, aloft with you. Take your glass and tell me what that signal is."

The signals midshipman was up the shrouds like a monkey and soon shouted down, "Signal reads 'Enemy in sight to north', sir."

Merriman took but a moment to decide what to do. "Lieutenant Merryweather, call the men to action stations and prepare to get under way. Have that signal repeated to *The Mayfly* and tell her to stand clear and move north away from us."

The marine drummer was there excitedly beating out the usual drum rolls as men poured up from below and ran to their positions. Mr Salmon, the gunner, was ready in his magazine - felt slippers on his feet - ready to hand out powder charges to the powder monkeys who would run up on deck with their dangerous load. Bangs and crashes sounded from below as a party of men removed cabin partitions and chests and furniture and took them down below.

The two lieutenants on the gun deck shouted almost together that their men were in position to starboard and larboard and guns ready to be loaded. There was a sudden silence as everyone and everything stood ready for what would happen next.

"Mr Green, what else can you see, any more sail?" shouted Merriman.

"No, sir, only *The Eagle*".

Damn it and blast it, thought Merriman standing by the taffrail. Here we are with our orders completed satisfactorily and ready to sail home and this happens. Surely it can only be a

French or Spanish ship in these waters. He paused in his thoughts as Peters brought his fighting sword and buckled it round his waist.

Another hail came from aloft. "*The Eagle* signalling, sir. Still enemy in sight and then another signal, a Spanish ship, sir."

Even as he spoke the masts of the enemy ship appeared over the horizon and rapidly drew nearer. All the officers were using telescopes and straining their eyes to try and identify the enemy.

"My God, sir, she's a big beast. Two rows of guns, a seventy four, I see," said Shrigley. "Can two frigates fight that?"

It was indeed huge and flying the colours of Spain. Lieutenant De Mowbray whispered, "'By the pricking of my thumbs, something evil this way comes'."

"An apt quotation, Lieutenant," said Merriman. "Macbeth, I think, but I have another. 'We would not seek a battle as we are, but as we are will not shun it'. That is from Henry the Fifth, I believe."

Chapter Twenty-Seven

The Spanish warship

Waiting for action is always the worst part, thought Merriman as he watched the Spanish warship approaching. Andrews had positioned *The Eagle* level with *Lord Stevenage,* but some distance away so that they could fight on either side of the enemy. Merriman looked round the quarterdeck at all the eager faces. His men were obviously looking forward to the encounter without thought that it could mean death or crippling or disfigurement.

"Another quotation, gentlemen, from Henry the Fifth again. It is, 'I see you stand like greyhounds in the slips, straining upon the start'. That seems to be an appropriate one, don't you think, Mr De Mowbray? Now I suggest you get yourself down on to the gundeck ready for action with your battery."

Unexpectedly, when the Spanish vessel was only half a mile away, she turned into the wind and fired each broadside one gun at a time when the British ships were not yet near. Merriman recognised that as an international signal of peaceful intentions, so he immediately ordered that *Lord Stevenage* backed the topsails and hove-to and her broadsides fired, knowing that all would be immediately reloaded. Captain Andrews in *The Eagle* followed suit. Out of the corner of his eye, Merriman noticed that the little brig *Mayfly,* now well to the north of the three ships had backed her tops'ls and was waiting.

"She's lowering a boat, sir. Two officers are going down into it and one seems to be carrying a white flag of truce," reported Lieutenant Shrigley. "I wonder what all this is about?"

"Mr Merryweather, I'll have all the gunports closed and have a small side party mustered, but remember the saying 'Bees that have honey in their mouths have a sting in their tails'."

"Sir, I think one of the two officers is the captain, at least I judge so by his gaudy uniform," called Shrigley.

Merriman had only one thought - that it must be news of the treaty - so he ordered that the side party greet the captain with full honours, piping and marines drawn up properly. "Peters," he shouted, "my hat and uniform coat, at once and bring Mr Humphries on deck."

The boat came swiftly alongside and, with oars tossed, touched by the boarding steps with hardly a bump.

"Well done," said Matthews. "That midshipman got it right. I doubt ours could do better."

The Spanish captain climbed up onto the deck and paused while the marines presented arms and the officers saluted with their swords. Then he raised his hat in acknowledgement and approached Merriman who was standing in front of his officers - obviously the captain.

"Señor, are you the Captain?" the man said in passable English. At Merriman's bow he said, "I have to tell you, Captain, that a peace treaty has been signed between France and England. That includes Spain as well, señor."

That phrase seemed to have been well rehearsed as the captain continued in voluble Spanish which fortunately Humphries could translate.

He introduced the two captains and, after bows were exchanged, Humphries said, "He tells us that he is Captain Alphonso and has brought documents to prove that what he said is true, sir. I told him your name."

"Very good, Mr Humphries. Invite him and the other officer down to my cabin and we can look at his documents." Merriman turned to Lieutenant Shrigley who was close by and whispered, "Keep your eye on that ship. If you see anything which might indicate she is preparing to fight, call me at once. Like us she has had time to load her guns again."

"Aye-aye, sir," replied the lieutenant.

Below in Merriman's great cabin, he asked Humphries to introduce himself and the first lieutenant to the two Spaniards. All bowed and Merriman waved them to the chairs surrounding the table which had been hastily brought up from the lower deck. "Mr Humphries, please ask them to show us the documents Captain Alphonso referred to." Whilst he did that Merriman signalled to the waiting Peters to bring brandy, which he produced immediately, having obviously expecting the order.

Humphries was reading the documents keenly and eventually raised his head and smiled. "All seems to be correct, sir. Once the Treaty – Treaty of Utrecht they call it - was signed they must have had an army of clerks copying it because it says here that hundreds of copies have been made for distribution to all Spanish, French and English possessions. Every ship has been given copies."

"Tell the captain, Mr Humphries, that I am happy that we do not have to fight as it would be difficult to foretell the outcome."

Much chatter ensued in Spanish and Merriman had to wait for a translation by Humphries.

"He says that he is happy too, sir, and he said that he remembers that a French ship of three decks was destroyed by two English frigates under Captain Edward Pellew. They drove the ship named *Droits de l'Homme* ashore where it became a total wreck with great loss of life. It seems that event has given him a healthy respect for the abilities of English ships."

"I remember it. Pellew commanded the frigate HMS *Indefatigable*. The other frigate the *Amazon* also went ashore in Audierne Bay, Plozévet if I recall. Tell him that the result could have been different if the French ship had not been prevented from opening her lower deck gunports because of the high seas. Now, enough of this idle talk, tell him that we captured a Spanish frigate weeks ago. *El Rey* or something like that and because we had little room for prisoners we put them ashore. Lieutenant Merryweather, please ask the master for the appropriate position."

Captain Alphonso looked horrified at the news and more excited talking ensued until Humphries said that the captain believed the men would be dead as the natives are so dangerous down that coast.

"Reassure him then and tell him that we left them with a

seaworthy boat, oars, sail and food and water and even some muskets and powder to defend themselves with, and tell him that I had suggested they sail south."

The Spaniard looked much relieved and when Merryweather returned and gave him a piece of paper with the master's calculation of where the men had been put ashore, he immediately asked to be excused as he felt that he should go at once to find them. And so he left. Within a couple of hours his ship was hull down on the horizon and Merriman's flotilla continued northwards.

Chapter Twenty-Eight

Home again to England

Twelve weeks later, the three ships arrived in Portsmouth after a slow and tedious voyage. At one point in the journey they had called in at Barbados to put the three French officers ashore where they might get passage somewhere on a French trading vessel - where to was up to them. Merriman explained the situation to the Admiral in command there and related the circumstances as to why they were on board *Lord Stevenage*.

"Well, Captain, we are no longer at war with France so it is of no concern to us what they do, but I imagine they would have difficulty explaining their situation back in Paris, don't you think?" the Admiral had said. "Now may I invite you and your captains to dinner this evening?"

"Thank you, sir, but no, we have to return back to report to the Treasury and the Admiralty as soon as we can. Mr Humphries here will explain why."

Humphries told the Admiral briefly what their mission to South America had been and that the documents were of the utmost importance to the government.

"Very well, gentlemen I will detain you no longer but what you will see when you arrive home I cannot say. I believe most of our fleet is being laid up in ordinary and the men paid off because of this damned treaty with France. Bonaparte will break it as soon as it suits him, mark my words, then where will we be?"

"I quite agree, sir. Once Mr Pitt left because of illness, Mr Addington has been only too eager to make treaty with Napoleon which Pitt would never have done."

"Well, you must be on your way, gentlemen. I expect I shall soon follow you as I'm too old to serve much more. I am looking forward to seeing my country estate again, not to mention my family. So may I wish you a fair voyage with a following wind."

At that they left the Admiral dreaming of retirement.

After an uneventful crossing back to England, it seemed to be no time at all before they were moving into Portsmouth harbour to anchor where ordered by the harbourmaster's boat. The harbour was full of warships and Merriman had never seen so much of England's naval might gathered together. Many of the ships seemed to have only recently arrived, salt-stained and battered, and others had already been de-commissioned and had their yards sent down in preparation for lying there in ordinary. Scores of boats were plying backwards and forward between the ships and the dockside, emptying the ships of anything that could go back into the naval stores.

Merriman, his captains and Mr Humphries made haste to present their reports to the Admiral in command of naval affairs, although he was too busy and preoccupied with problems to spare them much time.

"Take all personal possessions off, gentlemen, and see that the men are paid off. A pity, we are bound to need them again but they will have scattered. Then your ships can be laid up in ordinary," he said. "And you can be off to London, Captain and you Mr Humphries. I have received several messages from Admiral Sir Henry Goodwin at the Admiralty that you are to go there as soon as possible."

Back aboard the *Lord Stevenage,* Merriman, who had been thinking about the immediate future, asked Captains Andrews and Stewart and his own officers down to his cabin. There he supplied them with a drink and said, "So, gentlemen, our adventure has come to an end and we are to disperse. Who knows what the future will hold. I assume that all of you will be sent ashore with only half pay and you will go home. I am firm in my belief that this treaty with France will not last and we shall be called upon again. My reports about you and the junior officers are now in the hands of the Port Admiral. There is no more that I can do for you except to wish you well for the future and, if you should find yourselves in the Cheshire Wirral, I would be happy to see you. David, you have been to my home so you know where it is. So, gentlemen, it has been an honour to serve with you."

"Thank you, sir," they chorused and Stewart continued, "May I say that it has been an honour to serve with you, sir. I know I was a nuisance to you at first, but I have learned a lot and if I should be fortunate enough to be given another ship, I know I shall do better thanks to you."

"Well I do hope we shall meet again, gentlemen," said Merriman as he clasped hands with them in farewell. When they had gone, Merriman shouted, "Peters" and when the man appeared he asked him to fetch Matthews his cox'n and his clerk Tomkins to the cabin. When they arrived and stood in a nervous line before him, he said, "You know that the men of this ship are to be put ashore and paid off, so have you any idea what you will do, go to families perhaps?"

"No, sir," said Tomkins. "I have no home or family. I was begging when you found me so I suppose that is what I'll have to go back to. I won't find work, not heavy work anyway because of my old wound, sir."

"I see," Merriman replied. "And what about you, Peters?"

"I don't know, sir. As you know I daren't go ashore again here 'cos the justices were after me years ago for theft and embezzlement."

"And you, Matthews, what will you do?"

"Well, sir, I have no home to go to now. My wife died some years ago and we had no children, so I'll have to try and find a berth on a trading ship, sir."

"Hmm, I see. Now then, I'll tell you what I think you could do. If you are willing I will take you home with me to Burton where Peters can be my valet as I haven't got one. Tomkins, I'll find room for you to do something and Matthews, if you can steer a boat maybe you might manage to steer horses and be a coachman. Anyway when this treaty ends, as it will, I would want you with me aboard my next ship. What do you think of that?"

There was a moments' silence then they all tried to speak at once to thank him and with smiling faces said that they would be happy to do as he suggested.

"Good, good, I was hoping that that would be your reaction. Now once you are paid off I will give you money for the journey and entrust to you some of my possessions, including that wine holder that my wife gave to me. Tomkins, I appoint you treasurer; I'll give you the money. Peters, you know what I will have to take home. Matthews, you are a doughty fighting man so I rely on you to see that you all get there safely. Take pistols with you and a cutlass or two in case you meet footpads or highwaymen. One more thing, Tomkins, I want you to write out a letter authorising you all to be in charge of my possessions and why. I'll sign it before I leave for London in the morning. I will give you the money then too."

"Aye-aye, sir, we'll not let you down," and such other remarks they said with big grins on their faces.

"Now pass the word for all the crew to lay aft, I wish to speak with them."

When all the men were congregated aft in positions from which they could see him, Merriman stepped forward to the quarterdeck railing and said, "Men, as you know you will be paid off and this fine ship laid up in ordinary. But this treaty with France may not last and England will need her navy again. I have no doubt that I will be given another ship then and if you hear that and can make your way back to the navy, I would be pleased to see you back. I suggest you try and keep the uniform I supplied you with and wear it if you come back. Don't want the press picking you up, do we? So, thank you, men, for your service and loyalty and goodbye."

A voice shouted, "Three cheers for our captain, lads, 'an make 'em good uns." The cheers rang out and Merriman raised his hat in salute as other voices shouted, "We'll be back, sir, count on it," and other such sentiments.

Merriman was touched. He had to admit to himself that not many captains were as well regarded as he was, except he thought, Nelson himself. With another wave of his hat he retired below.

Chapter Twenty-Nine

A loving Reception at last

After a tiring but quick ten hour journey by poste-chaise, Merriman and Humphries arrived in London late in the day and were taken to the town house left to Merriman by his sponsor and friend Lord Stevenage, after whom his ship was named. There, the butler, Mr Garfield, was surprised to see them but welcomed them warmly. "It is good to see you again, Sir James. I'll have rooms ready for each of you in a moment." He rapidly organised the staff to light fires and bring hot water to the bedrooms and footmen to take their baggage there.

"My word, James," said Humphries. "This is a fine house – oh, I hope don't mind me calling you by your given name?"

"No I don't, sir, it should have happened long ago and I will use your name which I know to be George. Now we must wash and change before we have the meal which Mr Garfield tells me is being prepared."

Later, a footman knocked on their doors to tell them that the meal was ready. Afterwards they relaxed with a brandy apiece, with Humphries still looking round him surprised by the opulence of the house.

"Lord Stevenage left it to me, George. As you may know he had no family and I think he looked upon me as his son. He and my father were cousins after all."

In the morning, they were wakened by maids bringing hot water and footmen to assist, shaving them and helping with their clothing. Naturally Merriman was in his best uniform and Humphries in a very smart frock coat and, as they climbed into Lord Stevenage's small coach with Belton in the driving seat, Merriman reflected on how fortunate he was. The coach was now his and so was the house. He was really a very wealthy man.

Their first call was at East India House where Humphries was able to deliver the chest full of precious stones which were in fact the responsibility of the East India Company. Then on to the treasury where the long-awaited documents were delivered into the hands of Sir Laurence Grahame, the head of the English spy services. He immediately invited them to lunch with him. Merriman thanked him but demurred saying that he must report to the Admiralty at once, but would perhaps offer dinner at his town house later.

"Excellent, James, I look forward to that immensely and I'll bring Humphries with me."

At the Admiralty, Admiral Goodwin was eager to see him and Merriman was surprised at how quickly he was ushered into the Admiral's room.

"Good to see you again, Merriman, sit down and have a drink." He shouted for his harassed lieutenant to bring drinks in and continued with hardly a pause, "Were you successful in all respects, sir? The documents being the most important."

"It is all there in my report, Sir Henry," said Merriman, passing over a bulky packet of papers, "but briefly, sir, we very successful. We found Spanish ships rotting at anchor in Montevideo harbour and fired a broadside into them but Captain Andrews thought they would sink anyway as one had already done, they were so rotten. He then bombarded and set light to a good number of privateer ships there. He also captured the leader Don Carlos Galliano but he was killed by one of his Indian slaves and buried at sea. I most strongly recommend Captain Andrews to you, sir, he is a first rate officer."

Merriman continued to tell all that had happened: the destruction of the Spanish frigate, the destruction of the French frigate, the eventual recovery of the treasure and the important documents and the final meeting with the Spanish ship with news of the treaty.

The Admiral sat in silence for a few moments then asked, "What losses did you sustain, Captain?"

"Only two officers, sir. My Third Lieutenant Eric Bristow

and my Marine Lieutenant Charles Goodwin together with fifteen men."

The Admiral's face fell. "Bristow was my wife's sister's godson, she will miss him terribly, I know. Now, back to other matters. Of course you know that your ship and crew will be paid off, a foolish move if you ask me, so I suggest that you go home now and rest until that fool Addington comes to his senses or Pitt comes back and reinforces our navy. Then you will be needed again I'm sure."

That evening Merriman was ready for his guests who were announced by a rather pompous footman, "Sir Laurence Grahame, sir, and a Mr Humphries." They were served an excellent dinner and the conversation flowed between Merriman and Grahame as easily as it had done before between them at sea.

"There is a quotation, James," said Grahame, "from Othello I think, about drink which is 'O that men should put an enemy in their mouths to steal away their brains'. I think I have it right, but regardless of that, if I could have some more of your delicious claret?" He was quickly served by the waiting footman.

So a convivial evening passed and when his guests left, Merriman told Garfield to have his coach ready for an early start in the morning. "I think Belton the coachman should have a companion on the box and they should both have pistols at the ready."

Three days later the coach drew up in front of Merriman's home in Burton. A whirlwind of activity broke out when the coach was seen coming up the driveway. Servants poured out of the door and arranged themselves on the steps up to the house. The first to greet him was the new face of a man in a gold embellished frock coat. This man said, "Welcome home, Sir James. Her Ladyship has been informed and will be down immediately." He had hardly finished speaking before Merriman's wife Helen brushed him aside and, regardless of the servants, she threw herself into her husband's arms and they kissed and hugged each other passionately.

"Come inside, my love. Come inside and tell me and the children what you have been up to. I have so much to tell you about everything that I can hardly wait."

"It will have to, my dear. Who is this imposing personage?"

"Darkling is his name. I engaged him last year as our Major Domo or head of the house, James. I hope you approve."

"Very well, Darkling, send the coach men round to the back and have my luggage sent upstairs. I want to know that the coachmen are fed and rested and also the horses."

"Very good, Sir James. I shall attend to it instantly."

The rest of the day passed in excited chatter and playing with their children with hardly time to eat the fine meal prepared by the cook.

"What happened to Annie?" he asked Helen. Annie had been his mother's close friend for years and also the housekeeper and cook.

"I'm sorry, James, I should have told you, she died at the beginning of the year. She was a very old lady and the children miss her terribly. We buried her in the Burton churchyard, I'll show you tomorrow. I hired a nursery governess for the children."

"Very good, my love, and now I'm worn out from the journey so let us go to bed."

Worn out or not, Merriman acquitted himself nobly in his wife's arms and then fell asleep exhausted. He was vaguely aware of Helen shaking him awake in the morning and he was startled to find the sun blazing down and through the window.

"Darling, you slept like a log and the maid brought our breakfast up an hour ago. I sent her away to let you sleep as long as you could but I couldn't wait any longer to talk to you," she said. "And," she said, stroking his head, "I see you have a few grey hairs now. We can eat downstairs when we are ready, but not yet." Another bout of lovemaking and then Helen rang for hot water and for her maid to help her dress.

Merriman washed and shaved in a hurry and then dressed in a plain coat and trousers instead of his uniform. They had a good breakfast before Helen insisted in showing him the improvements she and the bailiff had made to the estate. At first he was awkward in the saddle but he enjoyed the ride in the fresh air.

Two days later a cart rumbled up the driveway to be sent round to the stable yard by an indignant Darkling, who then found Merriman to tell him that three strange men wished to see him.

Of course the men were Matthews, Peters and Tomkins with the cart full of Merriman's possessions.

"Good men, I'm pleased to see you. Now into the kitchen with you for a meal and I'll come with you. He led them into the kitchen where a startled cook and maids hastily curtseyed to him. "I want these three shipmates of mine to be fed with all they can eat and after that a footman can help them to unload the cart. Fall to, lads, I will see you later."

After all his goods had been brought into the house by his men and they had been fed, Merriman called Helen into the hall to introduce the three men to her. "This is my wife, Lady Helen, and Helen, this rogue is Matthews my cox'n whom I'm sure you remember. And this one is Peters who can give me the quickest and smoothest shave imaginable and I will keep him as my valet. And last is Tomkins, my clerk, a man badly injured at sea years ago and who has been invaluable in keeping the ship's books and paperwork in good order. I'm sure that we can find him something to do, perhaps to spare you some of the work you do with the estate records. They were all part of my crew and when I am called back to the fleet I will take them with me."

At mention of the fleet Helen's face fell, but she welcomed the men warmly and called to Darkling to find them suitable quarters.

"Thank you, my Lady," said Matthews, whom they seemed to have appointed their spokesman. "We'll try and do our best for you and the captain."

"I'm sure you will, Matthews," she said. "Mr Darkling will look after you until you have found your way about."

When they were alone, Helen's voice trembled as she said, "Are you going away again soon, James? I need more time with you."

He replied, "It all depends on that fellow Napoleon, my dear. We have this treaty which nobody expects him to keep to, but our foolish politicians have almost scrapped the navy. The general opinion is that Napoleon will keep to it for no longer than a year before he will be up to his old tricks again, trying to rule the world. So you see I could be home for a year or much less if their Lordships want me to go somewhere else."

In the event he was home for only seven or eight months before the letter Helen dreaded arrived from the Admiralty ordering him back to London, to take part in some new adventure.

THE END

Author Biography
Roger Burnage (1933 to 2015)

Roger Burnage had an eventful life that ultimately led him to pursue his passion for writing. Born and raised in the village of Lymm, Warrington, Cheshire, United Kingdom, he embarked on a journey of adventure and self-discovery.

Roger's life took an intriguing turn when he served in the Royal Air Force (RAF) during his national service. He was stationed in Ceylon, which is now known as Sri Lanka, where he worked as a radio mechanic, handling large transmitters.

After his release from the RAF, Roger went on to work as a draughtsman at Vickers in Manchester. Through dedication and hard work, he eventually climbed the ranks to become a sales engineer. His job involved traveling abroad to places like Scandinavia and India, which exposed him to new cultures and experiences.

It was during this period that Roger Burnage stumbled upon the Hornblower novels by C. S. Forester. The captivating tales of naval adventures ignited a spark of interest in the historical fiction genre within him.

Eventually, Roger settled in North Wales, where he focused on building a business and raising a family. Throughout his professional and personal life, the desire to write for himself never waned. However, it wasn't until retirement that he finally had the time and opportunity to pursue his dream of becoming an author.

Despite facing initial challenges and enduring multiple rejections from publishers and agents, Roger persevered. He refused to give up on his writing aspirations. Even when he underwent open-heart surgery and had an operation for a brain haemorrhage, he continued to work diligently on his craft. Typing away with only two fingers for months on end, he crafted "The Merriman Chronicles."

In 2012, with the support of his youngest son, Robin, Roger self-published his debut novel, "A Certain Threat," on Amazon KDP, making it available in both paperback and Kindle formats. His determination and talent began to bear fruit, as his fan base grew, and book sales remained strong.

More information about The Merriman Chronicles is available online

Follow the Authors on Amazon, and get notified when new books and audiobooks are released.

Desktop, Mobile & Tablet:
Search for the author, click the author's name on any of the book pages to jump to the Amazon author page, click the follow button at the bottom.

Kindle eReader and Kindle Apps:
The follow button is normally after the last page of the book.

For more background information, book details and announcements of upcoming novels, check the website at:

www.merriman-chronicles.com

You can also follow us on social media:-

https://twitter.com/Merriman1792

https://www.facebook.com/MerrimanChronicles

If you have enjoyed this novel, please leave a review or rating on Amazon or Goodreads. It genuinely helps.

Printed in Dunstable, United Kingdom